ROSINANTE
TO THE ROAD AGAIN

ROSINANTE
TO THE ROAD AGAIN

By
JOHN DOS PASSOS

ONESUCH PRESS

LONDON   MELBOURNE   NASHVILLE

Onesuch Press enriches lives by reclaiming the forgotten past; publishing the lesser known works of great authors and the great works of forgotten ones. For more information about us go to www.onesuchpress.com.

A ONESUCH book
Published by ONESUCH PRESS
PO Box 303BK, Black Hill 3350 Australia.

The first edition of John Dos Passos' *Rosinante to the Road Again* was published in 1922. This edition, first published in 2011 is based on that text. It has been reset with minor emendations.

National Library of Australia Cataloguing-in-Publication Entry
Author   Dos Passos, John, 1896-1970
ISBN   978 1 9871532-3-4 (paperback)
Title   Rosinante to the Road Again / by John Dos Passos
Dewey Number   814.52

Printed in the United States of America, the United Kingdom and Australia by Lightning Source, Inc.

The paper used in this publication meets the minimum requirements of ANSI/NISO Z39.48-1992 (R 1997) (Permanence of Paper). The paper used in this book is from responsibly managed forests.

CONTENTS

I	A GESTURE AND A QUEST	I
II	THE DONKEY BOY	11
III	THE BAKER OF ALMOROX	23
IV	TALK BY THE ROAD	34
V	A NOVELIST OF THE REVOLUTION	39
VI	TALK BY THE ROAD	50
VII	CORDOVA NO LONGER OF THE CALIPHS	52
VIII	TALK BY THE ROAD	58
IX	AN INVERTED MIDAS	61
X	TALK BY THE ROAD	68
XI	ANTONIO MACHADO; POET OF CASTILE	72
XII	A CATALAN POET	84
XIII	TALK BY THE ROAD	94
XIV	BENAVENTE'S MADRID	97
XV	TALK BY THE ROAD	105
XVI	A FUNERAL IN MADRID	108
XVII	TOLEDO	124

A GESTURE AND A QUEST

Telemachus had wandered so far in search of his father he had quite forgotten what he was looking for. He sat on a yellow plush bench in the café El Oro del Rhin, Plaza Santa Ana, Madrid, swabbing up with a bit of bread the last smudges of brown sauce off a plate of which the edges were piled with the dismembered skeleton of a pigeon. Opposite his plate was a similar plate his companion had already polished. Telemachus put the last piece of bread into his mouth, drank down a glass of beer at one spasmodic gulp, sighed, leaned across the table and said:

"I wonder why I'm here."

"Why anywhere else than here?" said Lyaeus, a young man with hollow cheeks and slow-moving hands, about whose mouth a faint pained smile was continually hovering, and he too drank down his beer.

At the end of a perspective of white marble tables, faces thrust forward over yellow plush cushions under twining veils of tobacco smoke, four German women on a little dais were playing *Tannhauser*. Smells of beer, sawdust, shrimps, roast pigeon.

"Do you know Jorge Manrique? That's one reason, Tel," the other man continued slowly. With one hand he gestured to the waiter for more beer, the other he waved across his face as if to brush away the music; then he recited, pronouncing the words haltingly:

> 'Recuerde el alma dormida,
> Avive el seso y despierte
> Contemplando
> Cómo se pasa la vida,
> Cómo se viene la muerte
> Tan callando:

Cuán presto se va el placer,
Cómo después de acordado
Da dolor,
Cómo a nuestro parecer
Cualquier tiempo pasado
Fué mejor.'

"It's always death," said Telemachus, "but we must go on."

It had been raining. Lights rippled red and orange and yellow and green on the clean paving-stones. A cold wind off the Sierra shrilled through clattering streets. As they walked, the other man was telling how this Castilian nobleman, courtier, man-at-arms, had shut himself up when his father, the Master of Santiago, died and had written this poem, created this tremendous rhythm of death sweeping like a wind over the world. He had never written anything else. They thought of him in the court of his great dust-colored mansion at Ocaña, where the broad eaves were full of a cooing of pigeons and the wide halls had dark rafters painted with arabesques in vermilion, in a suit of black velvet, writing at a table under a lemon tree. Down the sun-scarred street, in the cathedral that was building in those days, full of a smell of scaffolding and stone dust, there must have stood a tremendous catafalque where lay with his arms around him the Master of Santiago; in the carved seats of the choirs the stout canons intoned an endless growling litany; at the sacristy door, the flare of the candles flashing occasionally on the jewels of his mitre, the bishop fingered his crosier restlessly, asking his favorite choir-boy from time to time why Don Jorge had not arrived. And messengers must have come running to Don Jorge, telling him the service was on the point of beginning, and he must have waved them away with a grave gesture of a long white hand, while in his mind the distant sound of chanting, the jingle of the silver bit of his roan horse stamping nervously where he was tied to a twined Moorish column, memories of cavalcades filing with braying of trumpets and flutter of crimson damask into conquered towns, of court ladies dancing, and the noise of pigeons in the eaves, drew together like strings plucked in succession on a guitar into a great wave of rhythm in which his life was sucked away into this one poem in praise of death.

> Nuestras vidas son los ríos
> Que van a dar en la mar,
> Que es el morir....

Telemachus was saying the words over softly to himself as they went into the theatre. The orchestra was playing a Sevillana; as they found their seats they caught glimpses beyond people's heads and shoulders of a huge woman with a comb that pushed the tip of her mantilla a foot and a half above her head, dancing with ponderous dignity. Her dress was pink flounced with lace; under it the bulge of breasts and belly and three chins quaked with every thump of her tiny heels on the stage. As they sat down she retreated bowing like a full-rigged ship in a squall. The curtain fell, the theatre became very still; next was Pastora.

Strumming of a guitar, whirring fast, dry like locusts in a hedge on a summer day. Pauses that catch your blood and freeze it suddenly still like the rustling of a branch in silent woods at night. A gipsy in a red sash is playing, slouched into a cheap cane chair, behind him a faded crimson curtain. Off stage heels beaten on the floor catch up the rhythm with tentative interest, drowsily; then suddenly added, sharp click of fingers snapped in time; the rhythm slows, hovers like a bee over a clover flower. A little taut sound of air sucked in suddenly goes down the rows of seats. With faintest tapping of heels, faintest snapping of the fingers of a brown hand held over her head, erect, wrapped tight in yellow shawl where the embroidered flowers make a splotch of maroon over one breast, a flecking of green and purple over shoulders and thighs, Pastora Imperio comes across the stage, quietly, unhurriedly.

In the mind of Telemachus the words return:

> Cómo se viene la muerte
> Tan callando.

Her face is brown, with a pointed chin; her eyebrows that nearly meet over her nose rise in a flattened "A" towards the fervid black gleam of her hair; her lips are pursed in a half-smile as if she were stifling a secret. She walks round the stage slowly, one hand at her waist, the shawl tight over her elbow, her thighs lithe and restless, a panther in a cage. At the back of the stage she turns suddenly, advances; the snapping of her fingers gets loud, insistent; a thrill whirrs through the guitar like a covey of partridges scared in a field. Red heels tap threateningly.

> Decidme: la hermosura,
> La gentil frescura y tez
> De la cara
> El color y la blancura,
> Cuando viene la viejez
> Cuál se para?

She is right at the footlights; her face, brows drawn together into a frown, has gone into shadow; the shawl flames, the maroon flower over her breast glows like a coal. The guitar is silent, her fingers go on snapping at intervals with dreadful foreboding. Then she draws herself up with a deep breath, the muscles of her belly go taut under the tight silk wrinkles of the shawl, and she is off again, light, joyful, turning indulgent glances towards the audience, as a nurse might look in the eyes of a child she has unintentionally frightened with a too dreadful fairy story.

The rhythm of the guitar has changed again; her shawl is loose about her, the long fringe flutters; she walks with slow steps, in pomp, a ship decked out for a festival, a queen in plumes and brocade....

> ¿Qué se hicieron las damas,
> Sus tocados, sus vestidos,
> Sus olores?
> ¿Qué se hicieron las llamas
> De los fuegos encendidos
> De amadores?

And she has gone, and the gipsy guitar-player is scratching his neck with a hand the color of tobacco, while the guitar rests against his legs. He shows all his teeth in a world-engulfing yawn.

When they came out of the theatre, the streets were dry and the stars blinked in the cold wind above the houses. At the curb old women sold chestnuts and little ragged boys shouted the newspapers.

"And now do you wonder, Tel, why you are here?"

They went into a café and mechanically ordered beer. The seats were red plush this time and much worn. All about them groups of whiskered men leaning over tables, astride chairs, talking.

"It's the gesture that's so overpowering; don't you feel it in your arms? Something sudden and tremendously muscular."

"When Belmonte turned his back suddenly on the bull and walked away dragging the red cloak on the ground behind him I felt it," said Lyaeus.

"That gesture, a yellow flame against maroon and purple cadences ... an instant swagger of defiance in the midst of a litany to death the all-powerful. That is Spain.... Castile at any rate."

"Is 'swagger' the right word?"

"Find a better."

"For the gesture a medieval knight made when he threw his mailed glove at his enemy's feet or a rose in his lady's window, that a mule-driver makes when he tosses off a glass of aguardiente, that Pastora Imperio makes dancing.... Word! Rubbish!" And Lyaeus burst out laughing. He laughed deep in his throat with his head thrown back.

Telemachus was inclined to be offended.

"Did you notice how extraordinarily near she kept to the rhythm of Jorge Manrique?" he asked coldly.

"Of course. Of course," shouted Lyaeus, still laughing.

The waiter came with two mugs of beer.

"Take it away," shouted Lyaeus. "Who ordered beer? Bring something strong, champagne. Drink the beer yourself."

The waiter was scrawny and yellow, with bilious eyes, but he could not resist the laughter of Lyaeus. He made a pretense of drinking the beer.

Telemachus was now very angry. Though he had forgotten his

quest and the maxims of Penelope, there hovered in his mind a disquieting thought of an eventual accounting for his actions before a dimly imagined group of women with inquisitive eyes. This Lyaeus, he thought to himself, was too free and easy. Then there came suddenly to his mind the dancer standing tense as a caryatid before the footlights, her face in shadow, her shawl flaming yellow; the strong modulations of her torso seemed burned in his flesh. He drew a deep breath. His body tightened like a catapult.

"Oh to recapture that gesture," he muttered. The vague inquisitorial woman-figures had sunk fathoms deep in his mind.

Lyaeus handed him a shallow tinkling glass.

"There are all gestures," he said.

Outside the plate-glass window a countryman passed singing. His voice dwelt on a deep trembling note, rose high, faltered, skidded down the scale, then rose suddenly, frighteningly like a skyrocket, into a new burst of singing.

"There it is again," Telemachus cried. He jumped up and ran out on the street. The broad pavement was empty. A bitter wind shrilled among arc-lights white like dead eyes.

"Idiot," Lyaeus said between gusts of laughter when Telemachus sat down again. "Idiot Tel. Here you'll find it." And despite Telemachus's protestations he filled up the glasses. A great change had come over Lyaeus. His face looked fuller and flushed. His lips were moist and very red. There was an occasional crisp curl in the black hair about his temples.

And so they sat drinking a long while.

At last Telemachus got unsteadily to his feet.

"I can't help it…. I must catch that gesture, formulate it, do it. It is tremendously, inconceivably, unendingly important to me."

"Now you know why you're here," said Lyaeus quietly.

"Why are you here?"

"To drink," said Lyaeus.

"Let's go."

"Why?"

"To catch that gesture, Lyaeus," said Telemachus in an over-solemn voice.

"Like a comedy professor with a butterfly-net," roared Lyaeus. His laughter so filled the café that people at far-away tables smiled without knowing it.

"It's burned into my blood. It must be formulated, made permanent."

"Killed," said Lyaeus with sudden seriousness; "better drink it with your wine."

Silent they strode down an arcaded street. Cupolas, voluted baroque façades, a square tower, the bulge of a market building, tile roofs, chimneypots, ate into the star-dusted sky to the right and left of them, until in a great gust of wind they came out on an empty square, where were few gas-lamps; in front of them was a heavy arch full of stars, and Orion sprawling above it. Under the arch a pile of rags asked for alms whiningly. The jingle of money was crisp in the cold air.

"Where does this road go?"

"Toledo," said the beggar, and got to his feet. He was an old man, bearded, evil-smelling.

"Thank you…. We have just seen Pastora," said Lyaeus jauntily.

"Ah, Pastora!… The last of the great dancers," said the beggar, and for some reason he crossed himself.

The road was frosty and crunched silkily underfoot.

Lyaeus walked along shouting lines from the poem of Jorge Manrique.

> 'Cómo se pasa la vida
> Cómo se viene la muerte
> Tan callando:
> Cuán presto se va el placer
> Cómo después de acordado
> Da dolor,
> Cómo a nuestro parecer
> Cualquier tiempo pasado
> Fué mejor.'

"I bet you, Tel, they have good wine in Toledo."

The road hunched over a hill. They turned and saw Madrid cut out of darkness against the starlight. Before them sown plains, gulches full of mist, and the tremulous lights on many carts that jogged along, each behind three jingling slow mules. A cock crowed. All at once a voice burst suddenly in swaggering tremolo out of the darkness of the road beneath them, rising, rising, then fading off, then flaring up hotly like a red scarf waved on a windy day, like the swoop of a hawk, like a rocket intruding among the stars.

"Butterfly net, you old fool!" Lyaeus's laughter volleyed across the frozen fields.

Telemachus answered in a low voice:

"Let's walk faster."

He walked with his eyes on the road. He could see in the darkness, Pastora, wrapped in the yellow shawl with the splotch of maroon-colored embroidery moulding one breast, stand tremulous with foreboding before the footlights, suddenly draw in her breath, and turn with a great exultant gesture back into the rhythm of her dance. Only the victorious culminating instant of the gesture was blurred to him. He walked with long strides along the crackling road, his muscles aching for memory of it.

THE DONKEY BOY

II

Where the husbandman's toil and strife
Little varies to strife and toil:
But the milky kernel of life,
With her numbered: corn, wine, fruit, oil!

The path zigzagged down through the olive trees between thin chortling glitter of irrigation ditches that occasionally widened into green pools, reed-fringed, froggy, about which bristled scrub oleanders. Through the shimmer of olive leaves all about I could see the great ruddy heave of the mountains streaked with the emerald of millet-fields, and above, snowy shoulders against a vault of indigo, patches of wood cut out hard as metal in the streaming noon light. Tinkle of a donkey-bell below me, then at the turn of a path the donkey's hindquarters, mauve-grey, neatly clipped in a pattern of diamonds and lozenges, and a tail meditatively swishing as he picked his way among the stones, the head as yet hidden by the osier baskets of the pack. At the next turn I skipped ahead of the donkey and walked with the *arriero*, a dark boy in tight blue pants and short grey tunic cut to the waist, who had the strong cheek-bones, hawk nose and slender hips of an Arab, who spoke an aspirated Andalusian that sounded like Arabic.

We greeted each other cordially as travellers do in mountainous places where the paths are narrow. We talked about the weather and the wind and the sugar mills at Motril and women and travel and the vintage, struggling all the while like drowning men to understand each other's lingo. When it came out that I was an American and had been in the war, he became suddenly interested; of course, I was a deserter, he said, clever to get away. There'd been two deserters in his town a year ago, *Alemanes*; perhaps friends of mine. It was pointed out that I and the *Alemanes* had been at different ends of the gunbarrel. He laughed. What did that matter? Then he said several times, "Qué burro la guerra, qué burro la guerra." I remonstrated, pointing to the donkey that was following us with dainty steps, looking at us with a quizzical air from under his long eyelashes. Could anything be wiser than a burro?

He laughed again, twitching back his full lips to show the brilliance of tightly serried teeth, stopped in his tracks, and turned to look at the mountains. He swept a long brown hand across them. "Look," he said, "up there is the Alpujarras, the last refuge of the kings of the Moors; there are bandits up there sometimes. You have come to the right place; here we are free men."

The donkey scuttled past us with a derisive glance out of the corner of an eye and started skipping from side to side of the path, cropping here and there a bit of dry grass. We followed, the *arriero* telling how his brother would have been conscripted if the family had not got together a thousand pesetas to buy him out. That was no life for a man. He spat on a red stone. They'd never catch him, he was sure of that. The army was no life for a man.

In the bottom of the valley was a wide stream, which we forded after some dispute as to who should ride the donkey, the donkey all the while wrinkling his nose with disgust at the coldness of the speeding water and the sliminess of the stones. When we came out on the broad moraine of pebbles the other side of the stream we met a lean blackish man with yellow horse-teeth, who was much excited when he heard I was an American.

"America is the world of the future," he cried and gave me such a slap on the back I nearly tumbled off the donkey on whose rump I was at that moment astride.

"*En América no se divierte*," muttered the *arriero*, kicking his feet that were cold from the ford into the burning saffron dust of the road.

The donkey ran ahead kicking at pebbles, bucking, trying to shake off the big pear-shaped baskets of osier he had either side of his pack saddle, delighted with smooth dryness after so much water and such tenuous stony roads. The three of us followed arguing, the sunlight beating wings of white flame about us.

"In America there is freedom," said the blackish man, "there are no rural guards; roadmenders work eight hours and wear silk shirts and earn … un dineral." The blackish man stopped, quite out of breath from his grappling with infinity. Then he went on: "Your children are educated free, no priests, and at forty every man-jack owns an automobile."

"*Ca*," said the *arriero*.

"*Sí, hombre*," said the blackish man.

For a long while the *arriero* walked along in silence, watching his toes bury themselves in dust at each step. Then he burst out, spacing his words with conviction: "*Ca, en América no se hase na' a que trabahar y de'cansar.* … Not on your life, in America they don't do anything except work and rest so's to get ready to work again. That's no life for a man. People don't enjoy themselves there. An old sailor from Malaga who used to fish for sponges told me, and he knew. It's not gold people need, but bread and wine and … life. They don't do anything there except work and rest so they'll be ready to work again…."

Two thoughts jostled in my mind as he spoke; I seemed to see red-faced gentlemen in knee breeches, dog's-ear wigs askew over broad foreheads, reading out loud with unction the phrases, "inalienable rights … pursuit of happiness," and to hear the cadence out of Meredith's *The Day of the Daughter of Hades*:

> Where the husbandman's toil and strife
> Little varies to strife and toil:
> But the milky kernel of life,
> With her numbered: corn, wine, fruit, oil!

The donkey stopped in front of a little wineshop under a trellis where dusty gourd-leaves shut out the blue and gold dazzle of sun and sky.

"He wants to say, 'Have a little drink, gentlemen,'" said the blackish man.

In the greenish shadow of the wineshop a smell of anise and a sound of water dripping. When he had smacked his lips over a small cup of thick yellow wine he pointed at the *arriero*. "He says people don't enjoy life in America."

"But in America people are very rich," shouted the barkeeper, a beet-faced man whose huge girth was bound in a red cotton sash, and he made a gesture suggestive of coins, rubbing thumb and forefinger together.

Everybody roared derision at the *arriero*. But he persisted and went out shaking his head and muttering "That's no life for a man."

As we left the wineshop where the blackish man was painting with broad strokes the legend of the West, the *arriero* explained to me almost tearfully that he had not meant to speak ill of my country, but to explain why he did not want to emigrate. While he was speaking we passed a cartload of yellow grapes that drenched us in jingle of mulebells and in dizzying sweetness of bubbling ferment. A sombre man with beetling brows strode at the mule's head; in the cart, brown feet firmly planted in the steaming slush of grapes, flushed face tilted towards the ferocious white sun, a small child with a black curly pate rode in triumph, shouting, teeth flashing as if to bite into the sun.

"What you mean is," said I to the *arriero*, "that this is the life for a man."

He tossed his head back in a laugh of approval.

"Something that's neither work nor getting ready to work?"

"That's it," he answered, and cried, "*arrh he*" to the donkey.

We hastened our steps. My sweaty shirt bellied suddenly in the back as a cool wind frisked about us at the corner of the road.

"Ah, it smells of the sea," said the *arriero*. "We'll see the sea from the next hill."

That night as I stumbled out of the inn door in Motril, overfull of food and drink, the full moon bulged through the arches of the cupola of the pink and saffron church. Everywhere steel-green shadows striped with tangible moonlight. As I sat beside my knapsack in the *plaza*, groping for a thought in the bewildering dazzle of the night, three disconnected mules, egged on by a hoarse shouting, jingled out of the shadow. When they stopped with a jerk in the full moon-glare beside the fountain, it became evident that they were attached to a coach, a spidery coach tilted forward as if it were perpetually going down hill; from inside smothered voices like the strangled clucking of fowls being shipped to market in a coop.

On the driver's seat one's feet were on the shafts and one had a view of every rag and shoelace the harness was patched with. Creaking, groaning, with wabbling of wheels, grumble of inside passengers, cracking of whip and long strings of oaths from the driver, the coach lurched out of town and across a fat plain full of gurgle of irrigation ditches, shrilling of toads, falsetto rustle of broad leaves of the sugar cane. Occasionally the gleam of the soaring moon on banana leaves and a broad silver path on the sea. Landwards the hills like piles of ash in the moonlight, and far away a cloudy inkling of mountains.

Beside me, mouth open, shouting rich pedigrees at the leading mule, Cordovan hat on the back of his head, from under which sprouted a lock of black hair that hung between his eyes over his nose and made him look like a goblin, the driver bounced and squirmed and kicked at the flanks of the mules that roamed drunkenly from side to side of the uneven road. Down into a gulch, across a shingle, up over a plank bridge, then down again into the bed of the river I had forded that morning with my friend the *arriero*, along a beach with fishing boats and little huts where the fishermen slept; then barking of dogs, another bridge and we roared and crackled up a steep village street to come to a stop suddenly, catastrophically, in front of a tavern in the main square.

"We are late," said the goblin driver, turning to me suddenly, "I have not slept for four nights, dancing, every night dancing."

He sucked the air in through his teeth and stretched out his arms and legs in the moonlight. "Ah, women … women," he added philosophically. "Have you a cigarette?"

"Ah, la juventud," said the old man who had brought the mailbag. He looked up at us scratching his head. "It's to enjoy. A moment, a momentito, and it's gone! Old men work in the day time, but young men work at night.... Ay de mí," and he burst into a peal of laughter.

And as if some one were whispering them, the words of Jorge Manrique sifted out of the night:

>¿Qué se hizo el Rey Don Juan?
>Los infantes de Aragón
>¿Qué se hicieron?
>Qué fué de tanto galán,
>Qué fué de tanta invención,
>Cómo truxeron?

Everybody went into the tavern, from which came a sound of singing and of clapping in time, and as hearty a tinkle of glasses and banging on tables as might have come out of the *Mermaid* in the days of the Virgin Queen. Outside the moon soared, soared brilliant, a greenish blotch on it like the time-stain on a chased silver bowl on an altar. The broken lion's head of the fountain dribbled one tinkling stream of quicksilver. On the seawind came smells of rotting garbage and thyme burning in hearths and jessamine flowers. Down the street geraniums in a window smouldered in the moonlight; in the dark above them the merest contour of a face, once the gleam of two eyes; opposite against the white wall standing very quiet a man looking up with dilated nostrils—*el amor.*

As the coach jangled its lumbering unsteady way out of town, our ears still throbbed with the rhythm of the tavern, of hard brown hands clapped in time, of heels thumping on oak floors. From the last house of the village a man hallooed. With its noise of cupboards of china overturned the coach crashed to stillness. A wiry, white-faced man with a little waxed moustache like the springs of a mousetrap climbed on the front seat, while burly people heaved quantities of corded trunks on behind.

"How late, two hours late," the man spluttered, jerking his checked cap from side to side. "Since this morning nothing to eat

but two boiled eggs.... Think of that. *¡Qué incultura! ¡Qué pueblo
indecente!* All day only two boiled eggs."

"I had business in Motril, Don Antonio," said the goblin driver
grinning.

"Business!" cried Don Antonio, laughing squeakily, "and after all
what a night!"

Something impelled me to tell Don Antonio the story of King
Mycerinus of Egypt that Herodotus tells, how hearing from an
oracle he would only live ten years, the king called for torches and
would not sleep, so crammed twenty years' living into ten. The
goblin driver listened in intervals between his hoarse investigations
of the private life of the grandmother of the leading mule.

Don Antonio slapped his thigh and lit a cigarette and cried, "In
Andalusia we all do that, don't we, Paco?"

"Yes, sir," said the goblin driver, nodding his head vigorously.

"That is *lo flamenco*," cried Don Antonio. "The life of Andalusia is
lo flamenco."

The moon has begun to lose foothold in the black slippery zenith.
We are hurtling along a road at the top of a cliff; below the sea full
of unexpected glitters, lace-edged, swishing like the silk dress of a
dancer. The goblin driver rolls from side to side asleep. The check
cap is down over the little man's face so that not even his
moustaches are to be seen. All at once the leading mule, taken with
suicidal mania, makes a sidewise leap for the cliff-edge. Crumbling
of gravel, snap of traces, shouts, uproar inside. Some one has
managed to yank the mule back on her hind quarters. In the sea
below the shadow of a coach totters at the edge of the cliff's
shadow.

"Hija de puta," cries the goblin driver, jumping to the ground.

Don Antonio awakes with a grunt and begins to explain
querulously that he has had nothing to eat all day but two boiled
eggs. The teeth of the goblin driver flash white flame as he hangs
wreath upon wreath of profanity about the trembling, tugging
mules. With a terrific rattling jerk the coach sways to the safe side of

the road. From inside angry heads are poked out like the heads of hens out of an overturned coop. Don Antonio turns to me and shouts in tones of triumph: "¿Qué flamenco, eh?"

When we got to Almuñecar Don Antonio, the goblin driver, and I sat at a little table outside the empty Casino. A waiter appeared from somewhere with wine and coffee and tough purple ham and stale bread and cigarettes. Over our heads dusty palm-fronds trembled in occasional faint gusts off the sea. The rings on Don Antonio's thin fingers glistened in the light of the one tired electric light bulb that shone among palpitating mottoes above us as he explained to me the significance of *lo flamenco*.

The tough swaggering gesture, the quavering song well sung, the couplet neatly capped, the back turned to the charging bull, the mantilla draped with exquisite provocativeness; all that was *lo flamenco*. "On this coast, señor inglés, we don't work much, we are dirty and uninstructed, but by God we live. Why the poor people of the towns, d'you know what they do in summer? They hire a fig-tree and go and live under it with their dogs and their cats and their babies, and they eat the figs as they ripen and drink the cold water from the mountains, and man-alive they are happy. They fear no one and they are dependent on no one; when they are young they make love and sing to the guitar, and when they are old they tell stories and bring up their children. You have travelled much; I have travelled little—Madrid, never further,—but I swear to you that nowhere in the world are the women lovelier or is the land richer or the cookery more perfect than in this vega of Almuñecar…. If only the wine weren't quite so heavy…."

"Then you don't want to go to America?"

"¡Hombre por dios! Sing us a song, Paco…. He's a Galician, you see."

The goblin driver grinned and threw back his head.

"Go to the end of the world, you'll find a Gallego," he said. Then he drank down his wine, rubbed his mouth on the back of his hand, and started droningly:

'Si quieres qu'el carro cante
mójale y dejel'en río
que después de buen moja'o
canta com'un silbi'o.'

(If you want a cart to sing, wet it and soak it in the river, for when it's well soaked it'll sing like a locust.)

"Hola," cried Don Antonio, "go on."

'A mí me gusta el blanco,
¡viva lo blanco! ¡muera lo negro!
porque el negro es muy triste.
Yo soy alegre. Yo no lo quiero.'

(I like white; hooray for white, death to black. Because black is very sad, and I am happy, I don't like it.)

"That's it," cried Don Antonio excitedly. "You people from the north, English, Americans, Germans, whatnot, you like black. You like to be sad. I don't."

"'Yo soy alegre. Yo no lo quiero.'"

The moon had sunk into the west, flushed and swollen. The east was beginning to bleach before the oncoming sun. Birds started chirping above our heads. I left them, but as I lay in bed, I could hear the hoarse voice of the goblin driver roaring out:

'A mí me gusta el blanco,
¡viva lo blanco! ¡muera lo negro!'

At Nerja in an arbor of purple ipomoeas on a red jutting cliff over the beach where brown children were bathing, there was talk again of *lo flamenco*.

"In Spain," my friend Don Diego was saying, "we live from the belly and loins, or else from the head and heart: between *Don Quixote* the mystic and Sancho Panza the sensualist there is no middle ground. The lowest Panza is *lo flamenco*."

"But you do live."

"In dirt, disease, lack of education, bestiality.... Half of us are always dying of excess of food or the lack of it."

"What do you want?"

"Education, organization, energy, the modern world."

I told him what the donkey-boy had said of America on the road down from the Alpujarras, that in America they did nothing but work and rest so as to be able to work again. And America was the modern world.

And *lo flamenco* is neither work nor getting ready to work.

That evening San Miguel went out to fetch the Virgin of Sorrows from a roadside oratory and brought her back into town in procession with candles and skyrockets and much chanting, and as the swaying cone-shaped figure carried on the shoulders of six sweating men stood poised at the entrance to the *plaza* where all the girls wore jessamine flowers in the blackness of their hair, all waved their hats and cried, "¡*Viva la Virgen de las Angustias*!" And the Virgin and San Miguel both had to bow their heads to get in the church door, and the people followed them into the church crying "¡*Viva*!" so that the old vaults shivered in the tremulous candlelight and the shouting. Some people cried for water, as rain was about due and everything was very dry, and when they came out of the church they saw a thin cloud like a mantilla of white lace over the moon, so they went home happy.

Wherever they went through the narrow well-swept streets, lit by an occasional path of orange light from a window, the women left behind them long trails of fragrance from the jessamine flowers in their hair.

Don Diego and I walked a long while on the seashore talking of America and the Virgin and a certain soup called *ajo blanco* and *Don Quixote* and *lo flamenco*. We were trying to decide what was the peculiar quality of the life of the people in that rich plain (*vega* they call it) between the mountains of the sea. Walking about the country elevated on the small grass-grown levees of irrigation ditches, the owners of the fields we crossed used, simply because we were strangers, to offer us a glass of wine or a slice of watermelon. I had explained to my friend that in his modern world of America these same people would come out after us with shotguns loaded with rock salt. He answered that even so, the old order was changing, and that as there was nothing else but to follow the procession of industrialism it behooved Spaniards to see that their country forged ahead instead of being, as heretofore, dragged at the tail of the parade.

"And do you think it's leading anywhere, this endless complicating of life?"

"Of course," he answered.

"Where?"

"Where does anything lead? At least it leads further than *lo flamenco*."

"But couldn't the point be to make the way significant?"

He shrugged his shoulders. "Work," he said.

We had come to a little nook in the cliffs where fishing boats were drawn up with folded wings like ducks asleep. We climbed a winding path up the cliff. Pebbles scuttled underfoot; our hands were torn by thorny aromatic shrubs. Then we came out in a glen that cut far into the mountains, full of the laughter of falling water and the rustle of sappy foliage. Seven stilted arches of an aqueduct showed white through the canebrakes inland. Fragrances thronged about us; the smell of dry thyme-grown uplands, of rich wet fields, of goats, and jessamine and heliotrope, and of water cold from the snowfields running fast in ditches. Somewhere far off a donkey was braying. Then, as the last groan of the donkey faded, a man's voice rose suddenly out of the dark fields, soaring, yearning on taut throat-cords, then slipped down through notes, like a small boat sliding sideways down a wave, then unrolled a great slow scroll of rhythm on the night and ceased suddenly in an upward cadence as a guttering candle flares to extinction.

"Something that's neither work nor getting ready to work," and I thought of the *arriero* on whose donkey I had forded the stream on the way down from the Alpujarras, and his saying: "*Ca, en América no se hose na'a que trabahar y dé'cansar.*"

I had left him at his home village, a little cluster of red and yellow roofs about a fat tower the Moors had built and a gaunt church that hunched by itself in a square of trampled dust. We had rested awhile before going into town, under a fig tree, while he had put white canvas shoes on his lean brown feet. The broad leaves had rustled in the wind, and the smell of the fruit that hung purple bursting to crimson against the intense sky had been like warm stroking velvet all about us. And the *arriero* had discoursed on the merits of his donkey and the joys of going from town to town with merchandise, up into the mountains for chestnuts and firewood, down to the sea for fish, to Malaga for tinware, to Motril for sugar from the refineries. Nights of dancing and guitar-playing at vintage-time, fiestas of the Virgin, where older, realer gods were worshipped than Jehovah and the dolorous Mother of the pale Christ, the *toros*, blood and embroidered silks aflame in the sunlight, words whispered through barred windows at night, long days of travel on stony roads in the mountains…. And I had lain back with my eyes closed and the hum of little fig-bees in my ears, and wished that my life were his life. After a while we had jumped to our feet and I had shouldered my knapsack with its books and pencils and silly pads of paper and trudged off up an unshaded road, and had thought with a sort of bitter merriment of that prig Christian and his damned burden.

"Something that is neither work nor getting ready to work, to make the road so significant that one needs no destination, that is *lo flamenco*," said I to Don Diego, as we stood in the glen looking at the seven white arches of the aqueduct.

He nodded unconvinced.

III

I

The *señores* were from Madrid? Indeed! The man's voice was full of an awe of great distances. He was the village baker of Almorox, where we had gone on a Sunday excursion from Madrid; and we were standing on the scrubbed tile floor of his house, ceremoniously receiving wine and figs from his wife. The father of the friend who accompanied me had once lived in the same village as the baker's father, and bought bread of him; hence the entertainment. This baker of Almorox was a tall man, with a soft moustache very black against his ash-pale face, who stood with his large head thrust far forward. He was smiling with pleasure at the presence of strangers in his house, while in a tone of shy deprecating courtesy he asked after my friend's family. Don Fernando and Doña Ana and the Señorita were well? And little Carlos? Carlos was no longer little, answered my friend, and Doña Ana was dead.

The baker's wife had stood in the shadow looking from one face to another with a sort of wondering pleasure as we talked, but at this she came forward suddenly into the pale greenish-gold light that streamed through the door, holding a dark wine-bottle before her. There were tears in her eyes. No; she had never known any of them, she explained hastily—she had never been away from Almorox—but she had heard so much of their kindness and was sorry…. It was terrible to lose a father or a mother. The tall baker shifted his feet uneasily, embarrassed by the sadness that seemed slipping over his guests, and suggested that we walk up the hill to the Hermitage; he would show the way.

"But your work?" we asked. Ah, it did not matter. Strangers did not come every day to Almorox. He strode out of the door, wrapping a woolen muffler about his bare strongly moulded throat, and we followed him up the devious street of whitewashed houses that gave us glimpses through wide doors of dark tiled rooms with great black rafters overhead and courtyards where chickens pecked at the manure lodged between smooth worn flagstones. Still between white-washed walls we struck out of the village into the deep black mud of the high road, and at last burst suddenly into the open country, where patches of sprouting grass shone vivid green against the gray and russet of broad rolling lands. At the top of the first hill stood the Hermitage—a small whitewashed chapel with a square three-storied tower; over the door was a relief of the Virgin, crowned, in worn lichened stone. The interior was very plain with a single heavily gilt altar, over which was a painted statue, stiff but full of a certain erect disdainful grace—again of the Virgin. The figure was dressed in a long lace gown, full of frills and ruffles, grey with dust and age.

"*La Vírgen de la Cima*," said the baker, pointing reverently with his thumb, after he had bent his knee before the altar. And as I glanced at the image a sudden resemblance struck me: the gown gave the Virgin a curiously conical look that somehow made me think of that conical black stone, the Bona Dea, that the Romans brought from Asia Minor. Here again was a good goddess, a bountiful one, more mother than virgin, despite her prudish frills.... But the man was ushering us out.

"And there is no finer view than this in all Spain." With a broad sweep of his arm he took in the village below, with its waves of roofs that merged from green to maroon and deep crimson, broken suddenly by the open square in front of the church; and the gray towering church, scowling with strong lights and shadows on buttresses and pointed windows; and the brown fields faintly sheened with green, which gave place to the deep maroon of the turned earth of vineyards, and the shining silver where the wind ruffled the olive-orchards; and beyond, the rolling hills that grew gradually flatter until they sank into the yellowish plain of Castile. As he made the gesture his fingers were stretched wide as if to grasp all this land he was showing. His flaccid cheeks were flushed as he turned to us; but we should see it in May, he was saying, in May when the wheat was thick in the fields, and there were flowers on the hills. Then the lands were beautiful and rich, in May. And he went on to tell us of the local feast, and the great processions of the Virgin. This year there were to be four days of the *toros*. So many bullfights were unusual in such a small village, he assured us. But they were rich in Almorox; the wine was the best in Castile. Four days of *toros*, he said again; and all the people of the country around would come to the *fiestas*, and there would be a great pilgrimage to this Hermitage of the Virgin…. As he talked in his slow deferential way, a little conscious of his volubility before strangers, there began to grow in my mind a picture of his view of the world.

First came his family, the wife whose body lay beside his at night, who bore him children, the old withered parents who sat in the sun at his door, his memories of them when they had had strong rounded limbs like his, and of their parents sitting old and withered in the sun. Then his work, the heat of his ovens, the smell of bread cooking, the faces of neighbors who came to buy; and, outside, in the dim penumbra of things half real, of travellers' tales, lay Madrid, where the king lived and where politicians wrote in the newspapers,—and *Francia*—and all that was not Almorox…. In him I seemed to see the generations wax and wane, like the years, strung on the thread of labor, of unending sweat and strain of muscles against the earth. It was all so mellow, so strangely aloof from the modern world of feverish change, this life of the peasants of Almorox. Everywhere roots striking into the infinite past. For before the Revolution, before the Moors, before the Romans, before the dark furtive traders, the Phœnicians, they were much the same, these Iberian village communities. Far away things changed, cities were founded, hard roads built, armies marched and fought and passed away; but in Almorox the foundations of life remained unchanged up to the present. New names and new languages had come. The Virgin had taken over the festivals and rituals of the old earth goddesses, and the deep mystical fervor of devotion. But always remained the love for the place, the strong anarchistic reliance on the individual man, the walking, consciously or not, of the way beaten by generations of men who had tilled and loved and lain in the cherishing sun with no feeling of a reality outside of themselves, outside of the bare encompassing hills of their commune, except the God which was the synthesis of their souls and of their lives.

Here lies the strength and the weakness of Spain. This intense individualism, born of a history whose fundamentals lie in isolated village communities—*pueblos*, as the Spaniards call them—over the changeless face of which, like grass over a field, events spring and mature and die, is the basic fact of Spanish life. No revolution has been strong enough to shake it. Invasion after invasion, of Goths, of Moors, of Christian ideas, of the fads and convictions of the Renaissance, have swept over the country, changing surface customs and modes of thought and speech, only to be metamorphosed into keeping with the changeless Iberian mind.

And predominant in the Iberian mind is the thought *La vida es sueño*: "Life is a dream." Only the individual, or that part of life which is in the firm grasp of the individual, is real. The supreme expression of this lies in the two great figures that typify Spain for all time: Don Quixote and Sancho Panza; Don Quixote, the individualist who believed in the power of man's soul over all things, whose desire included the whole world in himself; Sancho, the individualist to whom all the world was food for his belly. On the one hand we have the ecstatic figures for whom the power of the individual soul has no limits, in whose minds the universe is but one man standing before his reflection, God. These are the Loyolas, the Philip Seconds, the fervid ascetics like Juan de la Cruz, the originals of the glowing tortured faces in the portraits of El Greco. On the other hand are the jovial materialists like the Archpriest of Hita, culminating in the frantic, mystical sensuality of such an epic figure as Don Juan Tenorio. Through all Spanish history and art the threads of these two complementary characters can be traced, changing, combining, branching out, but ever in substance the same. Of this warp and woof have all the strange patterns of Spanish life been woven.

II

In trying to hammer some sort of unified impression out of the scattered pictures of Spain in my mind, one of the first things I realize is that there are many Spains. Indeed, every village hidden in the folds of the great barren hills, or shadowed by its massive church in the middle of one of the upland plains, every fertile *huerta* of the seacoast, is a Spain. Iberia exists, and the strong Iberian characteristics; but Spain as a modern centralized nation is an illusion, a very unfortunate one; for the present atrophy, the desolating resultlessness of a century of revolution, may very well be due in large measure to the artificial imposition of centralized government on a land essentially centrifugal.

In the first place, there is the matter of language. Roughly, four distinct languages are at present spoken in Spain: Castilian, the language of Madrid and the central uplands, the official language, spoken in the south in its Andalusian form; Gallego-Portuguese, spoken on the west coast; Basque, which does not even share the Latin descent of the others; and Catalan, a form of Provençal which, with its dialect, Valencian, is spoken on the upper Mediterranean coast and in the Balearic Isles. Of course, under the influence of rail communication and a conscious effort to spread Castilian, the other languages, with the exception of Portuguese and Catalan, have lost vitality and died out in the larger towns; but the problem remains far different from that of the Italian dialects, since the Spanish languages have all, except Basque, a strong literary tradition.

Added to the variety of language, there is an immense variety of topography in the different parts of Spain. The central plateaux, dominant in modern history (history being taken to mean the births and breedings of kings and queens and the doings of generals in armor) probably approximate the warmer Russian steppes in climate and vegetation. The west coast is in most respects a warmer and more fertile Wales. The southern *huertas* (arable river valleys) have rather the aspect of Egypt. The east coast from Valencia up is a continuation of the Mediterranean coast of France. It follows that, in this country where an hour's train ride will take you from Siberian snow into African desert, unity of population is hardly to be expected.

Here is probably the root of the tendency in Spanish art and thought to emphasize the differences between things. In painting, where the mind of a people is often more tangibly represented than anywhere else, we find one supreme example. El Greco, almost the caricature in his art of the Don Quixote type of mind, who, though a Greek by birth and a Venetian by training, became more Spanish than the Spaniards during his long life at Toledo, strove constantly to express the difference between the world of flesh and the world of spirit, between the body and the soul of man. More recently, the extreme characterization of Goya's sketches and portraits, the intensifying of national types found in Zuloaga and the other painters who have been exploiting with such success the peculiarities—the picturesqueness—of Spanish faces and landscapes, seem to spring from this powerful sense of the separateness of things.

In another way you can express this constant attempt to differentiate one individual from another as caricature. Spanish art is constantly on the edge of caricature. Given the ebullient fertility of the Spanish mind and its intense individualism, a constant slipping over into the grotesque is inevitable. And so it comes to be that the conscious or unconscious aim of their art is rather self-expression than beauty. Their image of reality is sharp and clear, but distorted.

Burlesque and satire are never far away in their most serious moments. Not even the calmest and best ordered of Spanish minds can resist a tendency to excess of all sorts, to over-elaboration, to grotesquerie, to deadening mannerism. All that is greatest in their art, indeed, lies on the borderland of the extravagant, where sublime things skim the thin ice of absurdity. The great epic, Don Quixote, such plays as Calderon's *La Vida es Sueño*, such paintings as El Greco's *Resurrección* and Velasquez's dwarfs, such buildings as the Escorial and the Alhambra—all among the universal masterpieces—are far indeed from the middle term of reasonable beauty. Hence their supreme strength. And for our generation, to which excess is a synonym for beauty, is added argumentative significance to the long tradition of Spanish art.

Another characteristic, springing from the same fervid abundance, that links the Spanish tradition to ours of the present day is the strangely impromptu character of much Spanish art production. The slightly ridiculous proverb that genius consists of an infinite capacity for taking pains is well controverted. The creative flow of Spanish artists has always been so strong, so full of vitality, that there has been no time for taking pains. Lope de Vega, with his two thousand-odd plays—or was it twelve thousand?—is by no means an isolated instance. Perhaps the strong sense of individual validity, which makes Spain the most democratic country in Europe, sanctions the constant improvisation, and accounts for the confident planlessness as common in Spanish architecture as in Spanish political thought.

Here we meet the old stock characteristic, Spanish pride. This is a very real thing, and is merely the external shell of the fundamental trust in the individual and in nothing outside of him. Again El Greco is an example. As his painting progressed, grew more and more personal, he drew away from tangible reality, and, with all the dogmatic conviction of one whose faith in his own reality can sweep away the mountains of the visible world, expressed his own restless, almost sensual, spirituality in forms that flickered like white flames toward God. For the Spaniard, moreover, God is always, in essence, the proudest sublimation of man's soul. The same spirit runs through the preachers of the early church and the works of Santa Teresa, a disguise of the frantic desire to express the self, the self, changeless and eternal, at all costs. From this comes the hard cruelty that flares forth luridly at times. A recent book by Miguel de Unamuno, *Del Sentimiento Trágico de la Vida*, expresses this fierce clinging to separateness from the universe by the phrase *el hambre de inmortalidad*, the hunger of immortality. This is the core of the individualism that lurks in all Spanish ideas, the conviction that only the individual soul is real.

III

In the Spain of to-day these things are seen as through a glass, darkly. Since the famous and much gloated-over entrance of Ferdinand and Isabella into Granada, the history of Spain has been that of an attempt to fit a square peg in a round hole. In the great flare of the golden age, the age of ingots of Peru and of men of even greater worth, the disease worked beneath the surface. Since then the conflict has corroded into futility all the buoyant energies of the country. I mean the persistent attempt to centralize in thought, in art, in government, in religion, a nation whose every energy lies in the other direction. The result has been a deadlock, and the ensuing rust and numbing of all life and thought, so that a century of revolution seems to have brought Spain no nearer a solution of its problems. At the present day, when all is ripe for a new attempt to throw off the atrophy, a sort of despairing inaction causes the Spaniards to remain under a government of unbelievably corrupt and inefficient politicians. There seems no solution to the problem of a nation in which the centralized power and the separate communities work only to nullify each other.

Spaniards in face of their traditions are rather in the position of the archæologists before the problem of Iberian sculpture. For near the Cerro de los Santos, bare hill where from the ruins of a sanctuary has been dug an endless series of native sculptures of men and women, goddesses and gods, there lived a little watchmaker. The first statues to be dug up were thought by the pious country people to be saints, and saints they were, according to an earlier dispensation than that of Rome; with the result that much Kudos accompanied the discovery of those draped women with high head-dresses and fixed solemn eyes and those fragmentary bull-necked men hewn roughly out of grey stone; they were freed from the caked clay of two thousand years and reverently set up in the churches. So probably the motives that started the watchmaker on his career of sculpturing and falsifying were pious and reverential.

However it began, when it was discovered that the saints were mere horrid heathen he-gods and she-gods and that the foreign gentlemen with spectacles who appeared from all the ends of Europe to investigate, would pay money for them, the watchmaker began to thrive as a mighty man in his village and generation. He began to study archaeology and the style of his cumbersome forged divinities improved. For a number of years the statues from the Cerro de los Santos were swallowed whole by all learned Europe. But the watchmaker's imagination began to get the better of him; forms became more and more fantastic, Egyptian, Assyrian, *art-nouveau* influences began to be noted by the discerning, until at last someone whispered forgery and all the scientists scuttled to cover shouting that there had never been any native Iberian sculpture after all.

The little watchmaker succumbed before his imagining of heathen gods and died in a madhouse. To this day when you stand in the middle of the room devoted to the Cerro de los Santos in the Madrid, and see the statues of Iberian goddesses clustered about you in their high head-dresses like those of dancers, you cannot tell which were made by the watchmaker in 1880, and which by the image-maker of the hill-sanctuary at a time when the first red-eyed ships of the Phoenician traders were founding trading posts among the barbarians of the coast of Valencia. And there they stand on their shelves, the real and the false inextricably muddled, and stare at the enigma with stone eyes.

So with the traditions: the tradition of Catholic Spain, the tradition of military grandeur, the tradition of fighting the Moors, of suspecting the foreigner, of hospitality, of truculence, of sobriety, of chivalry, of Don Quixote and Tenorio.

The Spanish-American war, to the United States merely an opportunity for a patriotic-capitalist demonstration of sanitary engineering, heroism and canned-meat scandals, was to Spain the first whispered word that many among the traditions were false. The young men of that time called themselves the generation of ninety-eight. According to temperament they rejected all or part of the museum of traditions they had been taught to believe was the real Spain; each took up a separate road in search of a Spain which should suit his yearnings for beauty, gentleness, humaneness, or else vigor, force, modernity.

The problem of our day is whether Spaniards evolving locally, anarchically, without centralization in anything but repression, will work out new ways of life for themselves, or whether they will be drawn into the festering tumult of a Europe where the system that is dying is only strong enough to kill in its death-throes all new growth in which there was hope for the future. The Pyrenees are high.

IV

It was after a lecture at an exhibition of Basque painters in Madrid, where we had heard Valle-Melan, with eyes that burned out from under shaggy grizzled eyebrows, denounce in bitter stinging irony what he called the Europeanization of Spain. What they called progress, he had said, was merely an aping of the stupid commercialism of modern Europe. Better no education for the masses than education that would turn healthy peasants into crafty putty-skinned merchants; better a Spain swooning in her age-old apathy than a Spain awakened to the brutal soulless trade-war of modern life.... I was walking with a young student of philosophy I had met by chance across the noisy board of a Spanish *pensión*, discussing the exhibition we had just seen as a strangely meek setting for the fiery reactionary speech. I had remarked on the very "primitive" look much of the work of these young Basque painters had, shown by some in the almost affectionate technique, in the dainty caressing brush-work, in others by that inadequacy of the means at the painter's disposal to express his idea, which made of so many of the pictures rather gloriously impressive failures. My friend was insisting, however, that the primitiveness, rather than the birth-pangs of a new view of the world, was nothing but "the last affectation of an over-civilized tradition."

"Spain," he said, "is the most civilized country in Europe. The growth of our civilization has never been interrupted by outside influence. The Phoenicians, the Romans—Spain's influence on Rome was, I imagine, fully as great as Rome's on Spain; think of the five Spanish emperors;—the Goths, the Moors;—all incidents, absorbed by the changeless Iberian spirit.... Even Spanish Christianity," he continued, smiling, "is far more Spanish than it is Christian. Our life is one vast ritual. Our religion is part of it, that is all. And so are the bull-fights that so shock the English and Americans,—are they any more brutal, though, than fox-hunting and prize-fights? And how full of tradition are they, our *fiestas de toros*; their ceremony reaches back to the hecatombs of the Homeric heroes, to the bull-worship of the Cretans and of so many of the Mediterranean cults, to the Roman games. Can civilization go farther than to ritualize death as we have done? But our culture is too perfect, too stable. Life is choked by it."

We stood still a moment in the shade of a yellowed lime tree. My friend had stopped talking and was looking with his usual bitter smile at a group of little boys with brown, bare dusty legs who were intently playing bull-fight with sticks for swords and a piece of newspaper for the toreador's scarlet cape.

"It is you in America," he went on suddenly, "to whom the future belongs; you are so vigorous and vulgar and uncultured. Life has become once more the primal fight for bread. Of course the dollar is a complicated form of the food the cave man killed for and slunk after, and the means of combat are different, but it is as brutal. From that crude animal brutality comes all the vigor of life. We have none of it; we are too tired to have any thoughts; we have lived so much so long ago that now we are content with the very simple things,—the warmth of the sun and the colors of the hills and the flavor of bread and wine. All the rest is automatic, ritual."

"But what about the strike?" I asked, referring to the one-day's general strike that had just been carried out with fair success throughout Spain, as a protest against the government's apathy regarding the dangerous rise in the prices of food and fuel.

He shrugged his shoulders.

"That, and more," he said, "is new Spain, a prophecy, rather than a fact. Old Spain is still all-powerful."

Later in the day I was walking through the main street of one of the clustered adobe villages that lie in the folds of the Castilian plain not far from Madrid. The lamps were just being lit in the little shops where the people lived and worked and sold their goods, and women with beautifully shaped pottery jars on their heads were coming home with water from the well. Suddenly I came out on an open *plaza* with trees from which the last leaves were falling through the greenish sunset light. The place was filled with the lilting music of a grind-organ and with a crunch of steps on the gravel as people danced. There were soldiers and servant-girls, and red-cheeked apprentice-boys with their sweethearts, and respectable shop-keepers, and their wives with mantillas over their gleaming black hair. All were dancing in and out among the slim tree-trunks, and the air was noisy with laughter and little cries of childlike unfeigned enjoyment. Here was the gospel of Sancho Panza, I thought, the easy acceptance of life, the unashamed joy in food and color and the softness of women's hair. But as I walked out of the village across the harsh plain of Castile, grey-green and violet under the deepening night, the memory came to me of the knight of the sorrowful countenance, Don Quixote, blunderingly trying to remould the world, pitifully sure of the power of his own ideal. And in these two Spain seemed to be manifest. Far indeed were they from the restless industrial world of joyless enforced labor and incessant goading war. And I wondered to what purpose it would be, should Don Quixote again saddle Rosinante, and what the good baker of Almorox would say to his wife when he looked up from his kneading trough, holding out hands white with dough, to see the knight errant ride by on his lean steed upon a new quest.

IV

Telemachus and Lyaeus had walked all night. The sky to the east of them was rosy when they came out of a village at the crest of a hill. Cocks crowed behind stucco walls. The road dropped from their feet through an avenue of pollarded poplars ghostly with frost. Far away into the brown west stretched reach upon reach of lake-like glimmer; here and there a few trees pushed jagged arms out of drowned lands. They stood still breathing hard.

"It's the Tagus overflowed its banks," said Telemachus.

Lyaeus shook his head.

"It's mist."

They stood with thumping hearts on the hilltop looking over inexplicable shimmering plains of mist hemmed by mountains jagged like coals that as they looked began to smoulder with dawn. The light all about was lemon yellow. The walls of the village behind them were fervid primrose color splotched with shadows of sheer cobalt. Above the houses uncurled green spirals of wood-smoke.

Lyaeus raised his hands above his head and shouted and ran like mad down the hill. A little voice was whispering in Telemachus's ear that he must save his strength, so he followed sedately.

When he caught up to Lyaeus they were walking among twining wraiths of mist rose-shot from a rim of the sun that poked up behind hills of bright madder purple. A sudden cold wind-gust whined across the plain, making the mist writhe in a delirium of crumbling shapes. Ahead of them casting gigantic blue shadows over the furrowed fields rode a man on a donkey and a man on a horse. It was a grey sway-backed horse that joggled in a little trot with much switching of a ragged tail; its rider wore a curious peaked cap and sat straight and lean in the saddle. Over one shoulder rested a long bamboo pole that in the exaggerating sunlight cast a shadow like the shadow of a lance. The man on the donkey was shaped like a dumpling and rode with his toes turned out.

Telemachus and Lyaeus walked behind them a long while without catching up, staring curiously after these two silent riders.

Eventually getting as far as the tails of the horse and the donkey, they called out: *"Buenos días."*

There turned to greet them a red, round face, full of little lines like an over-ripe tomato and a long bloodless face drawn into a point at the chin by a grizzled beard.

"How early you are, gentlemen," said the tall man on the grey horse. His voice was deep and sepulchral, with an occasional flutter of tenderness like a glint of light in a black river.

"Late," said Lyaeus. "We come from Madrid on foot."

The dumpling man crossed himself.

"They are mad," he said to his companion.

"That," said the man on the grey horse, "is always the answer of ignorance when confronted with the unusual. These gentlemen undoubtedly have very good reason for doing as they do; and besides the night is the time for long strides and deep thoughts, is it not, gentlemen? The habit of vigil is one we sorely need in this distracted modern world. If more men walked and thought the night through there would be less miseries under the sun."

"But, such a cold night!" exclaimed the dumpling man.

"On colder nights than this I have seen children asleep in doorways in the streets of Madrid."

"Is there much poverty in these parts? asked Telemachus stiffly, wanting to show that he too had the social consciousness.

"There are people—thousands—who from the day they are born till the day they die never have enough to eat."

"They have wine," said Lyaeus.

"One little cup on Sundays, and they are so starved that it makes them as drunk as if it were a hogshead."

"I have heard," said Lyaeus, "that the sensations of starving are very interesting—people have visions more vivid than life."

"One needs very few sensations to lead life humbly and beautifully," said the man on the grey horse in a gentle tone of reproof.

Lyaeus frowned.

"Perhaps," said the man on the grey horse turning towards Telemachus his lean face, where under scraggly eyebrows glowered eyes of soft dark green, "it is that I have brooded too much on the injustice done in the world—all society one great wrong. Many years ago I should have set out to right wrong—for no one but a man, an individual alone, can right a wrong; organization merely substitutes one wrong for another—but now … I am too old. You see, I go fishing instead."

"Why, it's a fishing pole," cried Lyaeus. "When I first saw it I thought it was a lance." And he let out his roaring laugh.

"And such trout," cried the dumpling man. "The trout there are in that little stream above Illescas! That's why we got up so early, to fish for trout."

"I like to see the dawn," said the man on the grey horse.

"Is that Illescas?" asked Telemachus, and pointed to a dun brown tower topped by a cap of blue slate that stood guard over a cluster of roofs ahead of them. Telemachus had a map torn from Baedecker in his pocket that he had been peeping at secretly.

"That, gentlemen, is Illescas," said the man on the grey horse. "And if you will allow me to offer you a cup of coffee, I shall be most pleased. You must excuse me, for I never take anything before midday. I am a recluse, have been for many years and rarely stir abroad. I do not intend to return to the world unless I can bring something with me worth having." A wistful smile twisted a little the corners of his mouth.

"I could guzzle a hogshead of coffee accompanied by vast processions of toasted rolls in columns of four," shouted Lyaeus.

"We are on our way to Toledo," Telemachus broke in, not wanting to give the impression that food was their only thought.

"You will see the paintings of Dominico Theotocopoulos, the only one who ever depicted the soul of Castile."

"This man," said Lyaeus, with a slap at Telemachus's shoulder, "is looking for a gesture."

"The gesture of Castile."

The man on the grey horse rode along silently for some time. The sun had already burnt up the hoar-frost along the sides of the road; only an occasional streak remained glistening in the shadow of a ditch. A few larks sang in the sky. Two men in brown corduroy with hoes on their shoulders passed on their way to the fields.

"Who shall say what is the gesture of Castile?... I am from La Mancha myself." The man on the grey horse started speaking gravely while with a bony hand, very white, he stroked his beard. "Something cold and haughty and aloof...men concentrated, converging breathlessly on the single flame of their spirit.... Torquemada, Loyola, Jorge Manrique, Cortés, Santa Teresa.... Rapacity, cruelty, straightforwardness.... Every man's life a lonely ruthless quest."

Lyaeus broke in:

"Remember the infinite gentleness of the saints lowering the Conde de Orgaz into the grave in the picture in San Tomás...."

"Ah, that is what I was trying to think of.... These generations, my generation, my son's generation, are working to bury with infinite tenderness the gorgeously dressed corpse of the old Spain.... Gentlemen, it is a little ridiculous to say so, but we have set out once more with lance and helmet of knight-errantry to free the enslaved, to right the wrongs of the oppressed."

They had come into town. In the high square tower church-bells were ringing for morning mass. Down the broad main street scampered a flock of goats herded by a lean man with fangs like a dog who strode along in a snuff-colored cloak with a broad black felt hat on his head.

"How do you do, Don Alonso?" he cried; "Good luck to you, gentlemen." And he swept the hat off his head in a wide curving gesture as might a courtier of the Rey Don Juan.

The hot smell of the goats was all about them as they sat before the café in the sun under a bare acacia tree, looking at the tightly proportioned brick arcades of the mudéjar apse of the church opposite. Don Alonso was in the café ordering; the dumpling-man had disappeared. Telemachus got up on his numbed feet and stretched his legs. "Ouf," he said, "I'm tired." Then he walked over to the grey horse that stood with hanging head and drooping knees hitched to one of the acacias.

"I wonder what his name is." He stroked the horse's scrawny face. "Is it Rosinante?"

The horse twitched his ears, straightened his back and legs and pulled back black lips to show yellow teeth.

"Of course it's Rosinante!"

The horse's sides heaved. He threw back his head and whinnied shrilly, exultantly.

A NOVELIST OF REVOLUTION

I

Much as G.B.S. refuses to be called an Englishman, Pío Baroja refuses to be called a Spaniard. He is a Basque. Reluctantly he admits having been born in San Sebastián, outpost of Cosmopolis on the mountainous coast of Guipuzcoa, where a stern-featured race of mountaineers and fishermen, whose prominent noses, high ruddy cheek-bones and square jowls are gradually becoming known to the world through the paintings of the Zubiaurre, clings to its ancient un-Aryan language and its ancient song and customs with the hard-headedness of hill people the world over.

From the first Spanish discoveries in America till the time of our own New England clipper ships, the Basque coast was the backbone of Spanish trade. The three provinces were the only ones which kept their privileges and their municipal liberties all through the process of the centralizing of the Spanish monarchy with cross and faggot, which historians call the great period of Spain. The rocky inlets in the mountains were full of shipyards that turned out privateers and merchantmen manned by lanky broad-shouldered men with hard red-beaked faces and huge hands coarsened by generations of straining on heavy oars and halyards,—men who feared only God and the sea-spirits of their strange mythology and were a law unto themselves, adventurers and bigots.

It was not till the Nineteenth century that the Carlist wars and the passing of sailing ships broke the prosperous independence of the Basque provinces and threw them once for all into the main current of Spanish life. Now papermills take the place of shipyards, and instead of the great fleet that went off every year to fish the Newfoundland and Iceland banks, a few steam trawlers harry the sardines in the Bay of Biscay. The world war, too, did much to make Bilboa one of the industrial centers of Spain, even restoring in some measure the ancient prosperity of its shipping.

Pío Baroja spent his childhood on this rainy coast between green mountains and green sea. There were old aunts who filled his ears up with legends of former mercantile glory, with talk of sea captains and slavers and shipwrecks. Born in the late seventies, Baroja left the mist-filled inlets of Guipuzcoa to study medicine in Madrid, febrile capital full of the artificial scurry of government, on the dry upland plateau of New Castile. He even practiced, reluctantly enough, in a town near Valencia, where he must have acquired his distaste for the Mediterranean and the Latin genius, and, later, in his own province at Cestons, where he boarded with the woman who baked the sacramental wafers for the parish church, and, so he claims, felt the spirit of racial solidarity glow within him for the first time. But he was too timid in the face of pain and too sceptical of science as of everything else to acquire the cocksure brutality of a country doctor. He gave up medicine and returned to Madrid, where he became a baker. In *Juventud-Egolatria* ("Youth-Selfworship") a book of delightfully shameless self-revelations, he says that he ran a bakery for six years before starting to write. And he still runs a bakery.

You can see it any day, walking towards the Royal Theatre from the great focus of Madrid life, the Puerta del Sol. It has a most enticing window. On one side are hams and red sausages and purple sausages and white sausages, some plump to the bursting like Rubens's "Graces," others as weazened and smoked as saints by Ribera. In the middle are oblong plates with patés and sliced bologna and things in jelly; then come ranks of cakes, creamcakes and fruitcakes, everything from obscene jam-rolls to celestial cornucopias of white cream. Through the door you see a counter with round loaves of bread on it, and a basketful of brown rolls. If someone comes out a dense sweet smell of fresh bread and pastry swirls about the sidewalk.

So, by meeting commerce squarely in its own field, he has freed himself from any compromise with Mammon. While his bread remains sweet, his novels may be as bitter as he likes.

II

The moon shines coldly out of an intense blue sky where a few stars glisten faint as mica. Shadow fills half the street, etching a silhouette of roofs and chimneypots and cornices on the cobblestones, leaving the rest very white with moonlight. The façades of the houses, with their blank windows, might be carved out of ice. In the dark of a doorway a woman sits hunched under a brown shawl. Her head nods, but still she jerks a tune that sways and dances through the silent street out of the accordion on her lap. A little saucer for pennies is on the step beside her. In the next doorway two guttersnipes are huddled together asleep. The moonlight points out with mocking interest their skinny dirt-crusted feet and legs stretched out over the icy pavement, and the filthy rags that barely cover their bodies. Two men stumble out of a wineshop arm in arm, poor men in corduroy, who walk along unsteadily in their worn canvas shoes, making grandiloquent gestures of pity, tearing down the cold hard façades with drunken generous phrases, buoyed up by the warmth of the wine in their veins.

That is Baroja's world: dismal, ironic, the streets of towns where industrial life sits heavy on the neck of a race as little adapted to it as any in Europe. No one has ever described better the shaggy badlands and cabbage-patches round the edges of a city, where the debris of civilization piles up ramshackle suburbs in which starve and scheme all manner of human detritus. Back lots where men and women live fantastically in shelters patched out of rotten boards, of old tin cans and bits of chairs and tables that have stood for years in bright pleasant rooms. Grassy patches behind crumbling walls where on sunny days starving children spread their fleshless limbs and run about in the sun. Miserable wineshops where the wind whines through broken panes to chill men with ever-empty stomachs who sit about gambling and finding furious drunkenness in a sip of *aguardiente*. Courtyards of barracks where painters who have not a cent in the world mix with beggars and guttersnipes to cajole a little hot food out of soft-hearted soldiers at mess-time. Convent doors where ragged lines shiver for hours in the shrill wind that blows across the bare Castilian plain waiting for the nuns to throw out bread for them to fight over like dogs. And through it all moves the great crowd of the outcast, sneak-thieves, burglars, beggars of every description,—rich beggars and poor devils who have given up the struggle to exist,—homeless children, prostitutes, people who live a half-honest existence selling knicknacks, penniless students, inventors who while away the time they are dying of starvation telling all they meet of the riches they might have had; all who have failed on the daily treadmill of bread-making, or who have never had a chance even to enjoy the privilege of industrial slavery. Outside of Russia there has never been a novelist so taken up with all that society and respectability reject.

Not that the interest in outcasts is anything new in Spanish literature. Spain is the home of that type of novel which the pigeonhole-makers have named picaresque. These loafers and wanderers of Baroja's, like his artists and grotesque dreamers and fanatics, all are the descendants of the people in the *Quijote* and the *Novelas Ejemplares*, of the rogues and bandits of the Lazarillo de Tormes, who through *Gil Blas* invaded France and England, where they rollicked through the novel until Mrs. Grundy and George Eliot packed them off to the reform school. But the rogues of the seventeenth century were jolly rogues. They always had their tongues in their cheeks, and success rewarded their ingenious audacities. The moulds of society had not hardened as they have now; there was less pressure of hungry generations. Or, more probably, pity had not come in to undermine the foundations.

The corrosive of pity, which had attacked the steel girders of our civilization even before the work of building was completed, has brought about what Gilbert Murray in speaking of Greek thought calls the failure of nerve. In the seventeenth century men still had the courage of their egoism. The world was a bad job to be made the best of, all hope lay in driving a good bargain with the conductors of life everlasting. By the end of the nineteenth century the life everlasting had grown cobwebby, the French Revolution had filled men up with extravagant hopes of the perfectibility of this world, humanitarianism had instilled an abnormal sensitiveness to pain,—to one's own pain, and to the pain of one's neighbors. Baroja's outcasts are no longer jolly knaves who will murder a man for a nickel and go on their road singing "Over the hills and far away"; they are men who have not had the willpower to continue in the fight for bread, they are men whose nerve has failed, who live furtively on the outskirts, snatching a little joy here and there, drugging their hunger with gorgeous mirages.

One often thinks of Gorki in reading Baroja, mainly because of the contrast. Instead of the tumultuous spring freshet of a new race that drones behind every page of the Russian, there is the cold despair of an old race, of a race that lived long under a formula of life to which it has sacrificed much, only to discover in the end that the formula does not hold.

These are the last paragraphs of *Mala Hierba* ("Wild Grass"), the middle volume of Baroja's trilogy on the life of the very poor in Madrid.

"They talked. Manuel felt irritation against the whole world, hatred, up to that moment pent up within him against society, against man....

'Honestly,' he ended by saying, 'I wish it would rain dynamite for a week, and that the Eternal Father would come tumbling down in cinders.'

He invoked crazily all the destructive powers to reduce to ashes this miserable society.

Jesús listened with attention.

'You are an anarchist,' he told him.

'I?'

'Yes. So am I.'

'Since when?'

'Since I have seen the infamies committed in the world; since I have seen how coldly they give to death a bit of human flesh; since I have seen how men die abandoned in the streets and hospitals,' answered Jesús with a certain solemnity.

Manuel was silent. The friends walked without speaking round the Ronda de Segovia, and sat down on a bench in the little gardens of the Vírgen del Puerto.

The sky was superb, crowded with stars; the Milky Way crossed its immense blue concavity. The geometric figure of the Great Bear glittered very high. Arcturus and Vega shone softly in that ocean of stars.

In the distance the dark fields, scratched with lines of lights, seemed the sea in a harbor and the strings of lights the illumination of a wharf.

The damp warm air came laden with odors of woodland plants wilted by the heat.

'How many stars,' said Manuel. 'What can they be?'

'They are worlds, endless worlds.'

'I don't know why it doesn't make me feel better to see this sky so beautiful, Jesús. Do you think there are men in those worlds?' asked Manuel.

'Perhaps; why not?'

'And are there prisons too, and judges and gambling dens and police?... Do you think so?'

Jesús did not answer. After a while he began talking with a calm voice of his dream of an idyllic humanity, a sweet pitiful dream, noble and childish.

In his dream, man, led by a new idea, reached a higher state.

No more hatreds, no more rancours. Neither judges, nor police, nor soldiers, nor authority. In the wide fields of the earth free men worked in the sunlight. The law of love had taken the place of the law of duty, and the horizons of humanity grew every moment wider, wider and more azure.

And Jesús continued talking of a vague ideal of love and justice, of energy and pity; and those words of his, chaotic, incoherent, fell like balm on Manuel's ulcerated spirit. Then they were both silent, lost in their thoughts, looking at the night.

An august joy shone in the sky, and the vague sensation of space, of the infinity of those imponderable worlds, filled their spirits with a delicious calm."

III

Spain is the classic home of the anarchist. A bleak upland country mostly, with a climate giving all varieties of temperature, from moist African heat to dry Siberian cold, where people have lived until very recently,—and do still,—in villages hidden away among the bare ribs of the mountains, or in the indented coast plains, where every region is cut off from every other by high passes and defiles of the mountains, flaming hot in summer and freezing cold in winter, where the Iberian race has grown up centerless. The pueblo, the village community, is the only form of social cohesion that really has roots in the past. On these free towns empires have time and again been imposed by force. In the sixteenth and seventeenth centuries the Catholic monarchy wielded the sword of the faith to such good effect that communal feeling was killed and the Spanish genius forced to ingrow into the mystical realm where every ego expanded itself into the solitude of God. The eighteenth century reduced God to an abstraction, and the nineteenth brought pity and the mad hope of righting the wrongs of society. The Spaniard, like his own Don Quixote, mounted the warhorse of his idealism and set out to free the oppressed, alone. As a logical conclusion we have the anarchist who threw a bomb into the Lyceum Theatre in Barcelona during a performance, wanting to make the ultimate heroic gesture and only succeeding in a senseless mangling of human lives.

But that was the reduction to an absurdity of an immensely valuable mental position. The anarchism of Pío Baroja is of another sort. He says in one of his books that the only part a man of the middle classes can play in the reorganization of society is destructive. He has not undergone the discipline, which can only come from common slavery in the industrial machine, necessary for a builder. His slavery has been an isolated slavery which has unfitted him forever from becoming truly part of a community. He can use the vast power of knowledge which training has given him only in one way. His great mission is to put the acid test to existing institutions, and to strip the veils off them. I don't want to imply that Baroja writes with his social conscience. He is too much of a novelist for that, too deeply interested in people as such. But it is certain that a profound sense of the evil of existing institutions lies behind every page he has written, and that occasionally, only occasionally, he allows himself to hope that something better may come out of the turmoil of our age of transition.

Only a man who had felt all this very deeply could be so sensitive to the new spirit—if the word were not threadbare one would call it religious—which is shaking the foundations of the world's social pyramid, perhaps only another example of the failure of nerve, perhaps the triumphant expression of a new will among mankind.

In *Aurora Roja* ("Red Dawn"), the last of the Madrid trilogy, about the same Manuel who is the central figure of *Mala Hierba*, he writes:

"At first it bored him, but later, little by little, he felt himself carried away by what he was reading. First he was enthusiastic about Mirabeau; then about the Girondins; Vergniau Petion, Condorcet; then about Danton; then he began to think that Robespierre was the true revolutionary; afterwards Saint Just, but in the end it was the gigantic figure of Danton that thrilled him most....

Manuel felt great satisfaction at having read that history. Often he said to himself:

'What does it matter now if I am a loafer, and good-for-nothing? I've read the history of the French Revolution; I believe I shall know how to be worthy....'

After Michelet, he read a book about '48; then another on the Commune, by Louise Michel, and all this produced in him a great admiration for French Revolutionists. What men! After the colossal figures of the Convention: Babeuf, Proudhon, Blanqui, Bandin, Deleschize, Rochefort, Félix Pyat, Vallu.... What people!

'What does it matter now if I am a loafer?... I believe I shall know how to be worthy.'"

In those two phrases lies all the power of revolutionary faith. And how like phrases out of the gospels, those older expressions of the hope and misery of another society in decay. That is the spirit that, for good or evil, is stirring throughout Europe today, among the poor and the hungry and the oppressed and the outcast, a new affirmation of the rights and duties of men. Baroja has felt this profoundly, and has presented it, but without abandoning the function of the novelist, which is to tell stories about people. He is never a propagandist.

IV

"I have never hidden my admirations in literature. They have been and are Dickens, Balzac, Poe, Dostoievski and, now, Stendhal...." writes Baroja in the preface to the Nelson edition of *La Dama Errante* ("The Wandering Lady"). He follows particularly in the footprints of Balzac in that he is primarily a historian of morals, who has made a fairly consistent attempt to cover the world he lived in. With Dostoievski there is a kinship in the passionate hatred of cruelty and stupidity that crops out everywhere in his work. I have never found any trace of influence of the other three. To be sure there are a few early sketches in the manner of Poe, but in respect to form he is much more in the purely chaotic tradition of the picaresque novel he despises than in that of the American theorist.

Baroja's most important work lies in the four series of novels of the Spanish life he lived, in Madrid, in the provincial towns where he practiced medicine, and in the Basque country where he had been brought up. The foundation of these was laid by *El Arbol de la Ciencia* ("The Tree of Knowledge"), a novel half autobiographical describing the life and death of a doctor, giving a picture of existence in Madrid and then in two Spanish provincial towns. Its tremendously vivid painting of inertia and the deadening under its weight of intellectual effort made a very profound impression in Spain. Two novels about the anarchist movement followed it, *La Dama Errante*, which describes the state of mind of forward-looking Spaniards at the time of the famous anarchist attempt on the lives of the king and queen the day of their marriage, and *La Ciudad de la Niebla*, about the Spanish colony in London. Then came the series called *La Busca* ("The Search"), which to me is Baroja's best work, and one of the most interesting things published in Europe in the last decade. It deals with the lowest and most miserable life in Madrid and is written with a cold acidity which Maupassant would have envied and is permeated by a human vividness that I do not think Maupassant could have achieved. All three novels, *La Busca*, *Mala Hierba*, and *Aurora Roja*, deal with the drifting of a typical uneducated Spanish boy, son of a maid of all work in a boarding house, through different strata of Madrid life. They give a sense of unadorned reality very rare in any literature, and besides their power as novels are immensely interesting as sheer natural history. The type of the *golfo* is a literary discovery comparable with that of Sancho Panza by Cervántes.

Nothing that Baroja has written since is quite on the same level. The series *El Pasado* ("The Past") gives interesting pictures of provincial life. *Las Inquietudes de Shanti Andia* ("The Anxieties of Shanti Andia"), a story of Basque seamen which contains a charming picture of a childhood in a seaside village in Guipuzcoa, delightful as it is to read, is too muddled in romantic claptrap to add much to his fame. *El Mundo es Así* ("The World is Like That") expresses, rather lamely it seems to me, the meditations of a disenchanted revolutionist. The latest series, *Memorias de un Hombre de Acción*, a series of yarns about the revolutionary period in Spain at the beginning of the nineteenth century, though entertaining, is more an attempt to escape in a jolly romantic past the realities of the morose present than anything else. *César o Nada*, translated into English under the title of "Aut Cæsar aut Nullus" is also less acid and less effective than his earlier novels. That is probably why it was chosen for translation into English. We know how anxious our publishers are to furnish food easily digestible by weak American stomachs.

It is silly to judge any Spanish novelist from the point of view of form. Improvisation is the very soul of Spanish writing. In thinking back over books of Baroja's one has read, one remembers more descriptions of places and people than anything else. In the end it is rather natural history than dramatic creation. But a natural history that gives you the pictures etched with vitriol of Spanish life in the end of the nineteenth and the beginning of the twentieth century which you get in these novels of Baroja's is very near the highest sort of creation. If we could inject some of the virus of his intense sense of reality into American writers it would be worth giving up all these stale conquests of form we inherited from Poe and O. Henry. The following, again from the preface of *La Dama Errante*, is Baroja's own statement of his aims. And certainly he has realized them.

"Probably a book like la Dama Errante is not of the sort that lives very long; it is not a painting with aspirations towards the museum but an impressionist canvas; perhaps as a work it has too much asperity, is too hard, not serene enough.

This ephemeral character of my work does not displease me. We are men of the day, people in love with the passing moment, with all that is fugitive and transitory and the lasting quality of our work preoccupies us little, so little that it can hardly be said to preoccupy us at all."

VI

"Spain," said Don Alonso, as he and Telemachus walked out of Illescas, followed at a little distance by Lyaeus and the dumpling-man, "has never been swept clean. There have been the Romans and the Visigoths and the Moors and the French—armed men jingling over mountain roads. Conquest has warped and sterilised our Iberian mind without changing an atom of it. An example: we missed the Revolution and suffered from Napoleon. We virtually had no Reformation, yet the Inquisition was stronger with us than anywhere."

"Do you think it will have to be swept clean?" asked Telemachus.

"He does." Don Alonso pointed with a sweep of an arm towards a man working in the field beside the road. It was a short man in a blouse; he broke the clods the plow had left with a heavy triangular hoe. Sometimes he raised it only a foot above the ground to poise for a blow, sometimes he swung it from over his shoulder. Face, clothes, hands, hoe were brown against the brown hillside where a purple shadow mocked each heavy gesture with lank gesticulations. In the morning silence the blows of the hoe beat upon the air with muffled insistence.

"And he is the man who will do the building," went on Don Alonso; "It is only fair that we should clear the road."

"But you are the thinkers," said Telemachus; his mother Penelope's maxims on the subject of constructive criticism popped up suddenly in his mind like tickets from a cash register.

"Thought is the acid that destroys," answered Don Alonso.

Telemachus turned to look once more at the man working in the field. The hoe rose and fell, rose and fell. At a moment on each stroke a flash of sunlight came from it. Telemachus saw all at once the whole earth, plowed fields full of earth-colored men, shoulders thrown back, bent forward, muscles of arms swelling and slackening, hoes flashing at the same moment against the sky, at the same moment buried with a thud in clods. And he felt reassured as a traveller feels, hearing the continuous hiss and squudge of well oiled engines out at sea.

VII

When we stepped out of the bookshop the narrow street steamed with the dust of many carriages. Above the swiftly whirling wheels gaudily dressed men and women sat motionless in attitudes. Over the backs of the carriages brilliant shawls trailed, triangles of red and purple and yellow.

"Bread and circuses," muttered the man who was with me, "but not enough bread."

It was fair-time in Cordova; the carriages were coming back from the *toros*. We turned into a narrow lane, where the dust was yellow between high green and lavender-washed walls. From the street we had left came a sound of cheers and hand-clapping. My friend stopped still and put his hand on my arm.

"There goes Belmonte," he said; "half the men who are cheering him have never had enough to eat in their lives. The old Romans knew better; to keep people quiet they filled their bellies. Those fools—" he jerked his head backwards with disgust; I thought, of the shawls and the high combs and the hair gleaming black under lace and the wasp waists of the young men and the insolence of black eyes above the flashing wheels of the carriages, "—those fools give only circuses. Do you people in the outside world realize that we in Andalusia starve, that we have starved for generations, that those black bulls for the circuses may graze over good wheatland...to make Spain picturesque! The only time we see meat is in the bullring. Those people who argue all the time as to why Spain's backward and write books about it, I could tell them in one word: malnutrition." He laughed despairingly and started walking fast again. "We have solved the problem of the cost of living. We live on air and dust and bad smells."

I had gone into his bookshop a few minutes before to ask an address, and had been taken into the back room with the wonderful enthusiastic courtesy one finds so often in Spain. There the bookseller, a carpenter and the bookseller's errand-boy had all talked at once, explaining the last strike of farm-laborers, when the region had been for months under martial law, and they, and every one else of socialist or republican sympathies, had been packed for weeks into overcrowded prisons. They all regretted they could not take me to the Casa del Pueblo, but, they explained laughing, the Civil Guard was occupying it at that moment. It ended by the bookseller's coming out with me to show me the way to Azorín's.

Azorín was an architect who had supported the strikers; he had just come back to Cordova from the obscure village where he had been imprisoned through the care of the military governor who had paid him the compliment of thinking that even in prison he would be dangerous in Cordova. He had recently been elected municipal councillor, and when we reached his office was busy designing a schoolhouse. On the stairs the bookseller had whispered to me that every workman in Cordova would die for Azorín. He was a sallow little man with a vaguely sarcastic voice and an amused air as if he would burst out laughing at any moment. He put aside his plans and we all went on to see the editor of *Andalusia*, a regionalist pro-labor weekly.

In that dark little office, over three cups of coffee that appeared miraculously from somewhere with the pungent smell of ink and fresh paper in our nostrils, we talked about the past and future of Cordova, and of all the wide region of northern Andalusia, fertile irrigated plains, dry olive-land stretching up to the rocky waterless mountains where the mines are. In Azorín's crisp phrases and in the long ornate periods of the editor, the serfdom and the squalor and the heroic hope of these peasants and miners and artisans became vivid to me for the first time. Occasionally the compositor, a boy of about fifteen with a brown ink-smudged face, would poke his head in the door and shout: "It's true what they say, but they don't say enough, they don't say enough."

The problem in the south of Spain is almost wholly agrarian. From the Tagus to the Mediterranean stretches a mountainous region of low rainfall, intersected by several series of broad river-valleys which, under irrigation, are enormously productive of rice, oranges, and, in the higher altitudes, of wheat. In the dry hills grow grapes, olives and almonds. A country on the whole much like southern California. Under the Moors this region was the richest and most civilised in Europe.

When the Christian nobles from the north reconquered it, the ecclesiastics laid hold of the towns and extinguished industry through the Inquisition, while the land was distributed in huge estates to the magnates of the court of the Catholic Kings. The agricultural workers became virtually serfs, and the communal village system of working the land gradually gave way, Now the province of Jaen, certainly as large as the State of Rhode Island, is virtually owned by six families. This process was helped by the fact that all through the sixteenth and seventeenth centuries the liveliest people in all Spain swarmed overseas to explore and plunder America or went into the church, so that the tilling of the land was left to the humblest and least vigorous. And immigration to America has continued the safety valve of the social order.

It is only comparatively recently that the consciousness has begun to form among the workers of the soil that it is possible for them to change their lot. As everywhere else, Russia has been the beacon-flare. Since 1918 an extraordinary tenseness has come over the lives of the frugal sinewy peasants who, through centuries of oppression and starvation, have kept, in spite of almost complete illiteracy, a curiously vivid sense of personal independence. In the backs of taverns revolutionary tracts are spelled out by some boy who has had a couple of years of school to a crowd of men who listen or repeat the words after him with the fervor of people going through a religious mystery. Unspeakable faith possesses them in what they call "*la nueva ley*" ("the new law"), by which the good things a man wrings by his sweat from the earth shall be his and not the property of a distant señor in Madrid.

It is this hopefulness that marks the difference between the present agrarian agitation and the violent and desperate peasant risings of the past. As early as October, 1918, a congress of agricultural workers was held to decide on strike methods and, more important, to formulate a demand for the expropriation of the land. In two months the unions, (*"sociedades de resistencia"*) had been welded—at least in the province of Cordova—into a unified system with more or less central leadership. The strike which followed was so complete that in many cases even domestic servants went out. After savage repression and the military occupation of the whole province, the strike petered out into compromises which resulted in considerable betterment of working conditions but left the important issues untouched.

The rise in the cost of living and the growing unrest brought matters to a head again in the summer of 1919. The military was used with even more brutality than the previous year. Attempts at compromise, at parcelling out uncultivated land have proved as unavailing as the Mausers of the Civil Guard to quell the tumult. The peasants have kept their organizations and their demands intact. They are even willing to wait; but they are determined that the land upon which they have worn out generations and generations shall be theirs without question.

All this time the landlords brandish a redoubtable weapon: starvation. Already thousands of acres that might be richly fertile lie idle or are pasture for herds of wild bulls for the arena. The great land-owning families hold estates all over Spain; if in a given region the workers become too exigent, they decide to leave the land in fallow for a year or two. In the villages it becomes a question of starve or emigrate. To emigrate many certificates are needed. Many officials have to be placated. For all that money is needed. Men taking to the roads in search of work are persecuted as vagrants by the civil guards. Arson becomes the last retort of despair. At night the standing grain burns mysteriously or the country house of an absent landlord, and from the parched hills where gnarled almond-trees grow, groups of half starved men watch the flames with grim exultation.

Meanwhile the press in Madrid laments the *incultura* of the Andalusian peasants. The problem of civilization, after all, is often one of food calories. Fernando de los Ríos, socialist deputy for Granada, recently published the result of an investigation of the food of the agricultural populations of Spain in which he showed that only in the Balkans—out of all Europe—was the working man so under-nourished. The calories which the diet of the average Cordova workman represented was something like a fourth of those of the British workman's diet. Even so the foremen of the big estates complain that as a result of all this social agitation their workmen have taken to eating more than they did in the good old times.

How long it will be before the final explosion comes no one can conjecture. The spring of 1920, when great things were expected, was completely calm. On the other hand, in the last municipal elections when six hundred socialist councillors were elected in all Spain—in contrast to sixty-two in 1915—the vote polled in Andalusia was unprecedented. Up to this election many of the peasants had never dared vote, and those that had had been completely under the thumb of the *caciques*, the bosses that control Spanish local politics. However, in spite of socialist and syndicalist propaganda, the agrarian problem will always remain separate from anything else in the minds of the peasants. This does not mean that they are opposed to communism or cling as violently as most of the European peasantry to the habit of private property.

All over Spain one comes upon traces of the old communist village institutions, by which flocks and mills and bakeries and often land were held in common. As in all arid countries, where everything depends upon irrigation, ditches are everywhere built and repaired in common. And the idea of private property is of necessity feeble where there is no rain; for what good is land to a man without water? Still, until there grows up a much stronger community of interest than now exists between the peasants and the industrial workers, the struggle for the land and the struggle for the control of industry will be, in Spain, as I think everywhere, parallel rather than unified. One thing is certain, however long the fire smoulders before it flares high to make a clean sweep of Spanish capitalism and Spanish feudalism together, Cordova, hoary city of the caliphs, where ghosts of old grandeurs flit about the zigzag ochre-colored lanes, will, when the moment comes, be the center of organization of the agrarian revolution. When I was leaving Spain I rode with some young men who were emigrating to America, to make their fortunes, they said. When I told them I had been to Cordova, their faces became suddenly bright with admiration.

"Ah, Cordova," one of them cried; "they've got the guts in Cordova."

VIII

At the first crossroads beyond Illescas the dumpling-man and Don Alonso turned off in quest of the trout stream. Don Alonso waved solemnly to Lyaeus and Telemachus.

"Perhaps we shall meet in Toledo," he said.

"Catch a lot of fish," shouted Lyaeus.

"And perhaps a thought," was the last word they heard from Don Alonso.

The sun already high in the sky poured tingling heat on their heads and shoulders. There was sand in their shoes, an occasional sharp pain in their shins, in their bellies bitter emptiness.

"At the next village, Tel, I'm going to bed. You can do what you like," said Lyaeus in a tearful voice.

"I'll like that all right."

"*Buenos días, señores viajeros,*" came a cheerful voice. They found they were walking in the company of a man who wore a tight-waisted overcoat of a light blue color, a cream-colored felt hat from under which protruded long black moustaches with gimlet points, and shoes with lemon-yellow uppers. They passed the time of day with what cheerfulness they could muster.

"Ah, Toledo," said the man. "You are going to Toledo, my birthplace. There I was born in the shadow of the cathedral, there I shall die. I am a traveller of commerce." He produced two cards as large as postcards on which was written:

ANTONIO SILVA Y YEPES

UNIVERSAL AGENT

IMPORT EXPORT NATIONAL PRODUCTS

"At your service, gentlemen," he said and handed each of them a card. "I deal in tinware, ironware, pottery, lead pipes, enameled ware, kitchen utensils, American toilet articles, French perfumery, cutlery, linen, sewing machines, saddles, bridles, seeds, fancy poultry, fighting bantams and objects *de vertu*.... You are foreigners, are you not? How barbarous Spain, what people, what dirt, what lack of culture, what impoliteness, what lack of energy!"

The universal agent choked, coughed, spat, produced a handkerchief of crimson silk with which he wiped his eyes and mouth, twirled his moustaches and plunged again into a torrent of words, turning on Telemachus from time to time little red-rimmed eyes full of moist pathos like a dog's.

"Oh there are times, gentlemen, when it is too much to bear, when I rejoice to think that it's all up with my lungs and that I shan't live long anyway.... In America I should have been a Rockefeller, a Carnegie, a Morgan. I know it, for I am a man of genius. It is true. I am a man of genius.... And look at me here walking from one of these cursed tumbledown villages to another because I have not money enough to hire a cab.... And ill too, dying of consumption! O Spain, Spain, how do you crush your great men! What you must think of us, you who come from civilized countries, where life is organized, where commerce is a gentlemanly, even a noble occupation...."

"But you savor life more...."

"*Ca, ca,*" interrupted the universal agent with a downward gesture of the hand. "To think that they call by the same name living here in a pen like a pig and living in Paris, London, New York, Biarritz, Trouville ... luxurious beds, coiffures, toilettes, theatrical functions, sumptuous automobiles, elegant ladies glittering with diamonds ... the world of light and enchantment! Oh to think of it! And Spain could be the richest country in Europe, if we had energy, organization, culture! Think of the exports: iron, coal, copper, silver, oranges, hides, mules, olives, food products, woolens, cotton cloth, sugarcane, raw cotton ... couplets, dancers, gipsy girls...."

The universal agent had quite lost his breath. He coughed for a long time into his crimson handkerchief, then looked about him over the rolling dun slopes to which the young grain sprouting gave a sheen of vivid green like the patina on a Pompeian bronze vase, and shrugged his shoulders.

"*¡Qué vida!* What a life!"

For some time a spire had been poking up into the sky at the road's end; now yellow-tiled roofs were just visible humped out of the wheatland, with the church standing guard over them, it's buttresses as bowed as the legs of a bulldog. At the sight of the village a certain spring came back to Telemachus's fatigue-sodden legs. He noticed with envy that Lyaeus took little skips as he walked.

"If we properly exploited our exports we should be the richest people in Europe," the universal agent kept shouting with far-flung gestures of despair. And the last they heard from him as they left him to turn into the manure-littered, chicken-noisy courtyard of the Posada de la Luna was, "*¡Qué pueblo indecente!*... What a beastly town ... yet if they exploited with energy, with modern energy, their exports...."

AN INVERTED MIDAS

Every age must have had choice spirits whose golden fingers turned everything they touched to commonplace. Since we know our own literature best it seems unreasonably well equipped with these inverted Midases—though the fact that all Anglo-American writing during the last century has been so exclusively of the middle classes, by the middle classes and for the middle classes must count for something. Still Rome had her Marcus Aurelius, and we may be sure that platitudes would have obscured the slanting sides of the pyramids had stone-cutting in the reign of Cheops been as disastrously easy as is printing to-day. The addition of the typewriter to the printing-press has given a new and horrible impetus to the spread of half-baked thought. The labor of graving on stone or of baking tablets of brick or even of scrawling letters on paper with a pen is no longer a curb on the dangerous fluency of the inverted Midas. He now lolls in a Morris chair, sipping iced tea, dictating to four blonde and two dark-haired stenographers; three novels, a couple of books of travel and a short story written at once are nothing to a really enterprising universal genius. Poor Julius Caesar with his letters!

We complain that we have no supermen nowadays, that we can't live as much or as widely or as fervently or get through so much work as could Pico della Mirandola or Erasmus or Politian, that the race drifts towards mental and physical anæmia. I deny it. With the typewriter all these things shall be added unto us. This age too has its great universal geniuses. They overrun the seven continents and their respective seas. Accompanied by mænadic bands of stenographers, and a music of typewriters deliriously clicking, they go about the world, catching all the butterflies, rubbing the bloom off all the plums, tunneling mountains, bridging seas, smoothing the facets off ideas so that they may be swallowed harmlessly like pills. With true Anglo-Saxon conceit we had thought that our own Mr. Wells was the most universal of these universal geniuses. He has so diligently brought science, ethics, sex, marriage, sociology, God, and everything else—properly deodorized, of course—to the desk of the ordinary man, that he may lean back in his swivel-chair and receive faint susuration from the sense of progress and the complexity of life, without even having to go to the window to look at the sparrows sitting in rows on the telephone-wires, so that really it seemed inconceivable that anyone should be more universal. It was rumored that there lay the ultimate proof of Anglo-Saxon ascendancy. What other race had produced a great universal genius?

But all that was before the discovery of Blasco Ibáñez.

On the backs of certain of Blasco Ibáñez's novels published by the Casa Prometeo in Valencia is this significant advertisement: *Obras de Vulgarización Popular* ("Works of Popular Vulgarization"). Under it is an astounding list of volumes, all either translated or edited or arranged, if not written from cover to cover, by one tireless pen,—I mean typewriter. Ten volumes of universal history, three volumes of the French Revolution translated from Michelet, a universal geography, a social history, works on science, cookery and house-cleaning, nine volumes of Blasco Ibáñez's own history of the European war, and a translation of the Arabian Nights, a thousand and one of them without an hour missing. "Works of Popular Vulgarization." I admit that in Spanish the word *vulgarización* has not yet sunk to its inevitable meaning, but can it long stand such a strain? Add to that list a round two dozen novels and some books of travel, and who can deny that Blasco Ibáñez is a great universal genius? Read his novels and you will find that he has looked at the stars and knows Lord Kelvin's theory of vortices and the nebular hypothesis and the direction of ocean currents and the qualities of kelp and the direction the codfish go in Iceland waters when the northeast wind blows; that he knows about Gothic architecture and Byzantine painting, the social movement in Jerez and the exports of Patagonia, the wall-paper of Paris apartment houses and the red paste with which countesses polish their fingernails in Monte Carlo.

The very pattern of a modern major-general. And, like the great universal geniuses of the Renaissance, he has lived as well as thought and written. He is said to have been thirty times in prison, six times deputy; he has been a cowboy in the pampas of Argentina; he has founded a city in Patagonia with a bullring and a bust of Cervantes in the middle of it; he has rounded the Horn on a sailing-ship in a hurricane, and it is whispered that like Victor Hugo he eats lobsters with the shells on. He hobnobs with the universe.

One must admit, too, that Blasco Ibáñez's universe is a bulkier, burlier universe than Mr. Wells's. One is strangely certain that the axle of Mr. Wells's universe is fixed in some suburb of London, say Putney, where each house has a bit of garden where waddles an asthmatic pet dog, where people drink tea weak, with milk in it, before a gas-log, where every bookcase makes a futile effort to impinge on infinity through the encyclopedia, where life is a monotonous going and coming, swathed in clothes that must above all be respectable, to business and from business. But who can say where Blasco Ibáñez's universe centers? It is in constant progression.

Starting, as Walt Whitman from fish-shaped Paumonauk, from the fierce green fertility of Valencia, city of another great Spanish conqueror, the Cid, he had marched on the world in battle array. The whole history comes out in the series of novels at this moment being translated in such feverish haste for the edification of the American public. The beginnings are stories of the peasants of the fertile plain round about Valencia, of the fishermen and sailors of El Grao, the port, a sturdy violent people living amid a snappy fury of vegetation unexampled in Europe. His method is inspired to a certain extent by Zola, taking from him a little of the newspaper-horror mode of realism, with inevitable murder and sudden death in the last chapters. Yet he expresses that life vividly, although even then more given to grand vague ideas than to a careful scrutiny of men and things. He is at home in the strong communal feeling, in the individual anarchism, in the passionate worship of the water that runs through the fields to give life and of the blades of wheat that give bread and of the wine that gives joy, which is the moral make-up of the Valencian peasant. He is sincerely indignant about the agrarian system, about social inequality, and is full of the revolutionary bravado of his race.

A typical novel of this period is *La Barraca*, a story of a peasant family that takes up land which has lain vacant for years under the curse of the community, since the eviction of the tenants, who had held it for generations, by a landlord who was murdered as a result, on a lonely road by the father of the family he had turned out. The struggle of these peasants against their neighbours is told with a good deal of feeling, and the culmination in a rifle fight in an irrigation ditch is a splendid bit of blood and thunder. There are many descriptions of local customs, such as the Tribunal of Water that sits once a week under one of the portals of Valencia cathedral to settle conflicts of irrigation rights, a little dragged in by the heels, to be sure, but still worth reading. Yet even in these early novels one feels over and over again the force of that phrase "popular vulgarization." Valencia is being vulgarized for the benefit of the universe. The proletariat is being vulgarized for the benefit of the people who buy novels.

From Valencia raids seem to have been made on other parts of Spain. *Sonnica la Cortesana* gives you antique Saguntum and the usual "Aves," wreaths, flute-players and other claptrap of costume novels. In *La Catedral* you have Toledo, the church, socialism and the modern world in the shadow of Gothic spires. *La Bodega* takes you into the genial air of the wine vaults of Jerez-de-la-Frontera, with smugglers, processions blessing the vineyards and agrarian revolt in the background. Up to now they have been Spanish novels written for Spaniards; it is only with *Sangre y Arena* that the virus of a European reputation shows results.

In *Sangre y Arena*, to be sure, you learn that *toreros* use scent, have a home life, and are seduced by passionate Baudelairian ladies of the smart set who plant white teeth in their brown sinewy arms and teach them to smoke opium cigarettes. You see *toreros* taking the sacraments before going into the ring and you see them tossed by the bull while the crowd, which a moment before had been crying "hola" as if it didn't know that something was going wrong, gets very pale and chilly and begins to think what dreadful things *corridas* are anyway, until the arrival of the next bull makes them forget it. All of which is good fun when not obscured by grand, vague ideas, and incidentally sells like hot cakes. Thenceforward the Casa Prometeo becomes an exporting house dealing in the good Spanish products of violence and sunshine, blood, voluptuousness and death, as another vulgarizer put it.

Next comes the expedition to South America and *The Argonauts* appears. The Atlantic is bridged,—there open up rich veins of picturesqueness and new grand vague ideas, all in full swing when the war breaks out. Blasco Ibáñez meets the challenge nobly, and very soon, with *The Four Horsemen of the Apocalypse*, which captures the Allied world and proves again the *mot* about prophets. So without honor in its own country is the *Four Horsemen* that the English translation rights are sold for a paltry three thousand pesetas. But the great success in England and America soon shows that we can appreciate the acumen of a neutral who came in and rooted for our side; so early in the race too! While the iron is still hot another four hundred pages of well-sugared pro-Ally propaganda appears, *Mare Nostrum*, which mingles Ulysses and scientific information about ocean currents, Amphitrite and submarines, Circe and a vamping Theda Bara who was really a German Spy, in one grand chant of praise before the Mumbo-Jumbo of nationalism.

Los Enemigos de la Mujer, the latest production, abandons Spain entirely and plants itself in the midst of princes and countesses, all elaborately pro-Ally, at Monte Carlo. Forgotten the proletarian tastes of his youth, the local color he loved to lay on so thickly, the

Habañera atmosphere; only the grand vague ideas subsist in the cosmopolite, and the fluency, that fatal Latin fluency.

And now the United States, the home of the blonde stenographer and the typewriter and the press agent. What are we to expect from the combination of Blasco Ibáñez and Broadway?

At any rate the movies will profit.

Yet one can't help wishing that Blasco Ibáñez had not learnt the typewriter trick so early. Print so easily spins a web of the commonplace over the fine outlines of life. And Blasco Ibáñez need not have been an inverted Midas. His is a superbly Mediterranean type, with something of Arretino, something of Garibaldi, something of Tartarin of Tarascon. Blustering, sensual, enthusiastic, living at bottom in a real world—which can hardly be said of Anglo-Saxon vulgarizers—even if it is a real world obscured by grand vague ideas, Blasco Ibáñez's mere energy would have produced interesting things if it had not found such easy and immediate vent in the typewriter. Bottle up a man like that for a lifetime without means of expression and he'll produce memoirs equal to Marco Polo and Casanova, but let his energies flow out evenly without resistance through a corps of clicking typewriters and all you have is one more popular novelist.

It is unfortunate too that Blasco Ibáñez and the United States should have discovered each other at this moment. They will do each other no good. We have an abundance both of vague grand ideas and of popular novelists, and we are the favorite breeding place of the inverted Midas. We need writing that shall be acid, with sharp edges on it, yeasty to leaven the lump of glucose that the combination of the ideals of the man in the swivel-chair with decayed puritanism has made of our national consciousness. Of course Blasco Ibáñez in America will only be a seven days' marvel. Nothing is ever more than that. But why need we pretend each time that our seven days' marvels are the great eternal things?

Then, too, if the American public is bound to take up Spain it might as well take up the worth-while things instead of the works of popular vulgarization. They have enough of those in their bookcases as it is. And in Spain there is a novelist like Baroja, essayists like Unamuno and Azorín, poets like Valle Inclán and Antonio Machado, ... but I suppose they will shine with the reflected glory of the author of the *Four Horsemen* of the Apocalypse.

When they woke up it was dark. They were cold. Their legs were stiff. They lay each along one edge of a tremendously wide bed, between them a tangle of narrow sheets and blankets. Telemachus raised himself to a sitting position and put his feet, that were still swollen, gingerly to the floor. He drew them up again with a jerk and sat with his teeth chattering hunched on the edge of the bed. Lyaeus burrowed into the blankets and went back to sleep. For a long while Telemachus could not thaw his frozen wits enough to discover what noise had waked him up. Then it came upon him suddenly that huge rhythms were pounding about him, sounds of shaken tambourines and castanettes and beaten dish-pans and roaring voices. Someone was singing in shrill tremolo above the din a song of which each verse seemed to end with the phrase, "*y mañana Carnaval.*"

"Tomorrow's Carnival. Wake up," he cried out to Lyaeus, and pulled on his trousers.

Lyaeus sat up and rubbed his eyes.

"I smell wine," he said.

Telemachus, through hunger and stiffness and aching feet and the thought of what his mother Penelope would say about these goings on, if they ever came to her ears, felt a tremendous elation flare through him.

"Come on, they're dancing," he cried dragging Lyaeus out on the gallery that overhung the end of the court.

"Don't forget the butterfly net, Tel."

"What for?"

"To catch your gesture, what do you think?"

Telemachus caught Lyaeus by the shoulders and shook him. As

they wrestled they caught glimpses of the courtyard full of couples bobbing up and down in a *jota*. In the doorway stood two guitar players and beside them a table with pitchers and glasses and a glint of spilt wine. Feeble light came from an occasional little constellation of olive-oil lamps. When the two of them pitched down stairs together and shot out reeling among the dancers everybody cried out: "*Hola*," and shouted that the foreigners must sing a song.

"After dinner," cried Lyaeus as he straightened his necktie. "We haven't eaten for a year and a half!"

The *padrón*, a red thick-necked individual with a week's white bristle on his face, came up to them holding out hands as big as hams.

"You are going to Toledo for Carnival? O how lucky the young are, travelling all over the world." He turned to the company with a gesture; "I was like that when I was young."

They followed him into the kitchen, where they ensconced themselves on either side of a cave of a fireplace in which burned a fire all too small. The hunchbacked woman with a face like tanned leather who was tending the numerous steaming pots that stood about the hearth, noticing that they were shivering, heaped dry twigs on it that crackled and burst into flame and gave out a warm spicy tang.

"Tomorrow's Carnival," she said. "We mustn't stint ourselves." Then she handed them each a plate of soup full of bread in which poached eggs floated, and the *padrón* drew the table near the fire and sat down opposite them, peering with interest into their faces while they ate.

After a while he began talking. From outside the hand-clapping and the sound of castanettes continued interrupted by intervals of shouting and laughter and an occasional snatch from the song that ended every verse with "*y mañana Carnaval.*"

"I travelled when I was your age," he said. "I have been to America... Nueva York, Montreal, Buenos Aires, Chicago, San Francisco.... Selling those little nuts.... Yes, peanuts. What a country! How many laws there are there, how many policemen. When I was young I did not like it, but now that I am old and own an inn and daughters and all that, *vamos*, I understand. You see in Spain we all do just as we like; then, if we are the sort that goes to church we repent afterwards and fix it up with God. In European, civilized, modern countries everybody learns what he's got to do and what he must not do…. That's why they have so many laws…. Here the police are just to help the government plunder and steal all it wants…. But that's not so in America…."

"The difference is," broke in Telemachus, "as Butler put it, between living under the law and living under grace. I should rather live under gra…." But he thought of the maxims of Penelope and was silent.

"But after all we know how to sing," said the *Padrón*. "Will you have coffee with cognac?… And poets, man alive, what poets!"

The *padrón* stuck out his chest, put one hand in the black sash that held up his trousers and recited, emphasizing the rhythm with the cognac bottle:

'Aquí está Don Juan Tenorio;
no hay hombre para él …
Búsquenle los reñidores,
cérquenle los jugadores,
quien se précie que le ataje,
a ver si hay quien le aventaje
en juego, en lid o en amores.'

He finished with a flourish and poured more cognac into the coffee cups.

"*¡Que bonito!* How pretty!" cried the old hunchbacked woman who sat on her heels in the fireplace.

"That's what we do," said the *padrón*. "We brawl and gamble and seduce women, and we sing and we dance, and then we repent and the priest fixes it up with God. In America they live according to law."

Feeling well-toasted by the fire and well-warmed with food and drink, Lyaeus and Telemachus went to the inn door and looked out on the broad main street of the village where everything was snowy white under the cold stare of the moon. The dancing had stopped in the courtyard. A group of men and boys was moving slowly up the street, each one with a musical instrument. There were the two guitars, frying pans, castanettes, cymbals, and a goatskin bottle of wine that kept being passed from hand to hand. Each time the bottle made a round a new song started. And so they moved slowly up the street in the moonlight.

"Let's join them," said Lyaeus.

"No, I want to get up early so as...."

"To see the gesture by daylight!" cried Lyaeus jeeringly. Then he went on: "Tel, you live under the law. Under the law there can be no gestures, only machine movements."

Then he ran off and joined the group of men and boys who were singing and drinking. Telemachus went back to bed. On his way upstairs he cursed the maxims of his mother Penelope. But at any rate tomorrow, in Carnival-time, he would feel the gesture.

"I spent fifty thousand pesetas in a year at the military school....
J'aime le chic," said the young artillery officer of whom I had asked
the way. He was leading me up the steep cobbled hill that led to the
irregular main street of Segovia. A moment before we had passed
under the aqueduct that had soared above us arch upon arch into
the crimson sky. He had snapped tightly gloved fingers and said:
"And what's that good for, I'd like to know. I'd give it all for a puff
of gasoline from a Hispano-Suizo.... D'you know the Hispano-
Suizo? And look at this rotten town! There's not a street in it I can
speed on in a motorcycle without running down some fool old
woman or a squalling brat or other.... Who's this gentleman you are
going to see?"

"He's a poet," I said.

"I like poetry too. I write it ... light, elegant, about light elegant
women." He laughed and twirled the tiny waxed spike that stuck out
from each side of his moustache.

He left me at the end of the street I was looking for, and after an
elaborate salute walked off saying:

"To think that you should come here from New York to look for
an address in such a shabby street, and I so want to go to New
York. If I was a poet I wouldn't live here."

The name on the street corner was *Calle de los Desemparados*....
"Street of Abandoned Children."

We sat a long while in the casino, twiddling spoons in coffee-
glasses while a wax-pink fat man played billiards in front of us,
being ponderously beaten by a lean brownish swallow-tail with

yellow face and walrus whiskers that emitted a rasping *Bueno* after every play. There was talk of Paris and possible new volumes of verse, homage to Walt Whitman, Maragall, questioning about Emily Dickinson. About us was a smell of old horsehair sofas, a buzz of the poignant musty ennui of old towns left centuries ago high and dry on the beach of history. The group grew. Talk of painting: Zuloaga had not come yet, the Zubiaurre brothers had abandoned their Basque coast towns, seduced by the bronze-colored people and the saffron hills of the province of Segovia. Sorolla was dying, another had gone mad. At last someone said, "It's stifling here, let's walk. There is full moon tonight."

There was no sound in the streets but the irregular clatter of our footsteps. The slanting moonlight cut the street into two triangular sections, one enormously black, the other bright, engraved like a silver plate with the lines of doors, roofs, windows, ornaments. Overhead the sky was white and blue like buttermilk. Blackness cut across our path, then there was dazzling light through an arch beyond. Outside the gate we sat in a ring on square fresh-cut stones in which you could still feel a trace of the warmth of the sun. To one side was the lime-washed wall of a house, white fire, cut by a wide oaken door where the moon gave a restless glitter to the spiked nails and the knocker, and above the door red geraniums hanging out of a pot, their color insanely bright in the silver-white glare. The other side a deep glen, the shimmering tops of poplar trees and the sound of a stream. In the dark above the arch of the gate a trembling oil flame showed up the green feet of a painted Virgin. Everybody was talking about *El Buscón*, a story of Quevedo's that takes place mostly in Segovia, a wandering story of thieves and escapes by night through the back doors of brothels, of rope ladders dangling from the windows of great ladies, of secrets overheard in confessionals, and trysts under bridges, and fingers touching significantly in the holy-water fonts of tall cathedrals. A ghostlike wraith of dust blew through the gate. The man next me shivered.

"The dead are stronger than the living," he said. "How little we have; and they…."

In the quaver of his voice was a remembering of long muletrains jingling through the gate, queens in litters hung with patchwork curtains from Samarcand, gold brocades splashed with the clay of deep roads, stained with the blood of ambuscades, bales of silks from Valencia, travelling gangs of Moorish artisans, heavy armed Templars on their way to the Sepulchre, wandering minstrels, sneakthieves, bawds, rowdy strings of knights and foot-soldiers setting out with wine-skins at their saddlebows to cross the passes towards the debatable lands of Extremadura, where there were infidels to kill and cattle to drive off and village girls to rape, all when the gate was as new and crisply cut out of clean stone as the blocks we were sitting on. Down in the valley a donkey brayed long and dismally.

"They too have their nostalgias," said someone sentimentally.

"What they of the old time did not have," came a deep voice from under a bowler hat, "was the leisure to be sad. The sweetness of putrefaction, the long remembering of palely colored moods; they had the sun, we have the colors of its setting. Who shall say which is worth more?"

The man next to me had got to his feet. "A night like this with a moon like this," he said, "we should go to the ancient quarter of the witches."

Gravel crunched under our feet down the road that led out of moonlight into the darkness of the glen—to *San Millán de las brujas*.

You cannot read any Spanish poet of today without thinking now and then of Rubén Darío, that prodigious Nicaraguan who collected into his verse all the tendencies of poetry in France and America and the Orient and poured them in a turgid cataract, full of mud and gold-dust, into the thought of the new generation in Spain. Overflowing with beauty and banality, patched out with images and ornaments from Greece and Egypt and France and Japan and his own Central America, symbolist and romantic and Parnassian all at once, Rubén Darío's verse is like those doorways of the Spanish Renaissance where French and Moorish and Italian motives jostle in headlong arabesques, where the vulgarest routine stone-chipping is interlocked with designs and forms of rare beauty and significance. Here and there among the turgid muddle, out of the impact of unassimilated things, comes a spark of real poetry. And that spark can be said—as truly as anything of the sort can be said—to be the motive force of the whole movement of renovation in Spanish poetry. Of course the poets have not been content to be influenced by the outside world only through Darío. Baudelaire and Verlaine had a very large direct influence, once the way was opened, and their influence succeeded in curbing the lush impromptu manner of romantic Spanish verse. In Antonio Machado's work—and he is beginning to be generally considered the central figure—there is a restraint and terseness of phrase rare in any poetry.

I do not mean to imply that Machado can be called in any real sense a pupil of either Darío or Verlaine; rather one would say that in a generation occupied largely in more or less unsuccessful imitation of these poets, Machado's poetry stands out as particularly original and personal. In fact, except for the verse of Juan Ramón Jiménez, it would be in America and England rather than in Spain, in Aldington and Amy Lowell, that one would find analogous aims and methods. The influence of the symbolists and the turbulent experimenting of the Nicaraguan broke down the bombastic romantic style current in Spain, as it was broken down everywhere else in the middle nineteenth century. In Machado's work a new method is being built up, that harks back more to early ballads and the verse of the first moments of the Renaissance than to anything foreign, but which shows the same enthusiasm for the rhythms of ordinary speech and for the simple pictorial expression of undoctored emotion that we find in the renovators of poetry the world over. *Campos de Castilla*, his first volume to be widely read, marks an epoch in Spanish poetry.

Antonio Machado's verse is taken up with places. It is obsessed with the old Spanish towns where he has lived, with the mellow sadness of tortuous streets and of old houses that have soaked up the lives of generations upon generations of men, crumbling in the flaming silence of summer noons or in the icy blast off the mountains in winter. Though born in Andalusia, the bitter strength of the Castilian plain, where half-deserted cities stand aloof from the world, shrunken into their walls, still dreaming of the ages of faith and conquest, has subjected his imagination, and the purity of Castilian speech has dominated his writing, until his poems seem as Castilian as Don Quixote.

> "My childhood: memories of a courtyard in Seville,
> and of a bright garden where lemons hung ripening.
> My youth: twenty years in the land of Castile.
> My history: a few events I do not care to remember."

So Machado writes of himself. He was born in the eighties, has been a teacher of French in government schools in Soria and Baeza and at present in Segovia—all old Spanish cities very mellow and very stately—and has made the migration to Paris customary with Spanish writers and artists. He says in the *Poema de un Día*:

> Here I am, already a teacher
> of modern languages, who yesterday
> was a master of the gai scavoir
> and the nightingale's apprentice.

He has published three volumes of verse, *Soledades* ("Solitudes"), *Campos de Castilla* ("Fields of Castile"), and *Soledades y Galerías* ("Solitudes and Galleries"), and recently a government institution, the Residencia de Estudiantes, has published his complete works up to date.

The following translations are necessarily inadequate, as the poems depend very much on modulations of rhythm and on the expressive fitting together of words impossible to render in a foreign language. He uses rhyme comparatively little, often substituting assonance in accordance with the peculiar traditions of Spanish prosody. I have made no attempt to imitate his form exactly.

I

Yes, come away with me—fields of Soria,
quiet evenings, violet mountains,
aspens of the river, green dreams
of the grey earth,
bitter melancholy
of the crumbling city—
perhaps it is that you have become
the background of my life.
Men of the high Numantine plain,
who keep God like old—Christians,
may the sun of Spain fill you
with joy and light and abundance!

II

A frail sound of a tunic trailing
across the infertile earth,
and the sonorous weeping
of the old bells.
The dying embers
of the horizon smoke.
White ancestral ghosts
go lighting the stars.
—Open the balcony-window. The hour
of illusion draws near...
The afternoon has gone to sleep
and the bells dream.

III

Figures in the fields against the sky!
Two slow oxen plough
on a hillside early in autumn,
and between the black heads bent down
under the weight of the yoke,
hangs and sways a basket of reeds,
a child's cradle;
And behind the yoke stride
a man who leans towards the earth

and a woman who, into the open furrows,
throws the seed.
Under a cloud of carmine and flame,
in the liquid green gold of the setting,
their shadows grow monstrous.

IV

Naked is the earth
and the soul howls to the wan horizon
like a hungry she-wolf.
What do you seek,
poet, in the sunset?
Bitter going, for the path
weighs one down, the frozen wind,
and the coming night and the bitterness
of distance…. On the white path
the trunks of frustrate trees show black,
on the distant mountains
there is gold and blood. The sun dies….
What do you seek,
poet, in the sunset?

V

Silver hills and grey ploughed lands,
violet outcroppings of rock
through which the Duero traces
its curve like a cross-bow
about Soria,
dark oak-wood, wild cliffs,
bald peaks,
and the white roads and the aspens of the river.

Afternoons of Soria, mystic and warlike,
today I am very sad for you,
sadness of love,
Fields of Soria,
where it seems that the rocks dream,
come with me! Violet rocky outcroppings,
silver hills and grey ploughed lands.

VI

We think to create festivals
of love out of our love,
to burn new incense
on untrodden mountains;
and to keep the secret
of our pale faces,
and why in the bacchanals of life
we carry empty glasses,
while with tinkling echoes and laughing
foams the gold must of the grape....
A hidden bird among the branches
of the solitary park
whistles mockery.... We feel
the shadow of a dream in our wine-glass,
and something that is earth in our flesh
feels the dampness of the garden like a caress.

VII

I have been back to see the golden aspens,
aspens of the road along the Duero
between San Polo and San Saturio,
beyond the old stiff walls
of Soria, barbican
towards Aragon of the Castilian lands.
These poplars of the river, that chime
when the wind blows their dry leaves
to the sound of the water,
have in their bark the names of lovers,
initials and dates.
Aspens of love where yesterday
the branches were full of nightingales,
aspens that tomorrow will sing
under the scented wind of the springtime,
aspens of love by the water
that speeds and goes by dreaming,
aspens of the bank of the Duero,
come away with me.

VIII

Cold Soria, clear Soria,
key of the outlands,
with the warrior castle
in ruins beside the Duero,
and the stiff old walls,
and the blackened houses.

Dead city of barons
and soldiers and huntsmen,
whose portals bear the shields
of a hundred hidalgos;
city of hungry greyhounds,
of lean greyhounds
that swarm
among the dirty lanes
and howl at midnight
when the crows caw.

Cold Soria! The clock
of the Lawcourts has struck one.
Soria, city of Castile,
so beautiful under the moon.

IX AT A FRIEND'S BURIAL

They put him away in the earth
a horrible July afternoon
under a sun of fire.

A step from the open grave
grew roses with rotting petals
among geraniums of bitter fragrance,
red-flowered. The sky
a pale blue. A wind
hard and dry.

Hanging on the thick ropes,
the two gravediggers
let the coffin heavily
down into the grave.

It struck the bottom with a sharp sound,
solemnly, in the silence.

The sound of a coffin striking the earth
is something unutterably solemn.
The heavy clods broke into dust
over the black coffin.
A white mist of dust rose in the air
out of the deep grave.
And you, without a shadow now, sleep.
Long peace to your bones.
For all time
you sleep a tranquil and a real sleep.

X THE IBERIAN GOD

Like the cross-bowman,
the gambler in the song,
the Iberian had an arrow for his god
when he shattered the grain with hail
and ruined the fruits of autumn;
and a gloria when he fattened
the barley and the oats
that were to make bread tomorrow.
"God of ruin,
I worship because I wait and because I fear.
I bend in prayer to the earth
a blasphemous heart.
"Lord, through whom I snatch my bread with pain,
I know your strength, I know my slavery.
Lord of the clouds in the east
that trample the country-side,
of dry autumns and late frosts
and of the blasts of heat that scorch the harvests!
"Lord of the iris in the green meadows
where the sheep graze,
Lord of the fruit the worms gnaw
and of the hut the whirlwind shatters,
your breath gives life to the fire in the hearth,
your warmth ripens the tawny grain,
and your holy hand, St. John's eve,
hardens the stone of the green olive.

"Lord of riches and poverty,
Of fortune and mishap,
who gives to the rich luck and idleness,
and pain and hope to the poor!

"Lord, Lord, in the inconstant wheel
of the year I have sown my sowing
that has an equal chance with the coins
of a gambler sown on the gambling-table!

"Lord, a father today, though stained with yesterday's blood,
two-faced of love and vengeance,
to you, dice cast into the wind,
goes my prayer, blasphemy and praise!"

This man who insults God in his altars,
without more care of the frown of fate,
also dreamed of paths across the seas
and said: "It is God who walks upon the waters."

Is it not he who put God above war,
beyond fate,
beyond the earth,
beyond the sea and death?

Did he not give the greenest bough
of the dark-green Iberian oak
for God's holy bonfire,
and for love flame one with God?

But today ... What does a day matter?
for the new household gods
there are plains in forest shade
and green boughs in the old oak-woods.

Though long the land waits
for the curved plough to open the first furrow,
there is sowing for God's grain
under thistles and burdocks and nettles.

What does a day matter? Yesterday waits
for tomorrow, tomorrow for infinity;
men of Spain, neither is the past dead,
nor is tomorrow, nor yesterday, written.

Who has seen the face of the Iberian God?
I wait for the Iberian man who with strong hands

will carve out of Castilian oak
The parched God of the grey land.

A Catalan Poet

XII

It is time for sailing; the swallow has come chattering and the mellow west wind; the meadows are already in bloom; the sea is silent and the waves the rough winds pummeled. Up anchors and loose the hawsers, sailor, set every stitch of canvas. This I, Priapos the harbor god, command you, man, that you may sail for all manner of ladings. (Leonidas in the Greek Anthology.)

Catalonia like Greece is a country of mountains and harbors, where the farmers and herdsmen of the hills can hear in the morning the creak of oars and the crackling of cordage as the great booms of the wing-shaped sails are hoisted to the tops of the stumpy masts of the fishermen's boats. Barcelona with its fine harbor nestling under the towering slopes of Montjuic has been a trading city since most ancient times. In the middle ages the fleets of its stocky merchants were the economic scaffolding which underlay the pomp and heraldry of the great sea kingdom of the Aragonese. To this day you can find on old buildings the arms of the kings of Aragon and the counts of Barcelona in Mallorca and Manorca and Ibiza and Sardinia and Sicily and Naples. It follows that when Catalonia begins to reëmerge as a nucleus of national consciousness after nearly four centuries of subjection to Castile, poets speaking Catalan, writing Catalan, shall be poets of the mountains and of the sea.

Yet this time the motor force is not the sailing of white argosies towards the east. It is textile mills, stable, motionless, drawing about them muddled populations, raw towns, fattening to new arrogance the descendants of those stubborn burghers who gave the kings of Aragon and of Castile such vexing moments. (There's a story of one king who was so chagrined by the tight-pursed contrariness of the Cortes of Barcelona that he died of a broken heart in full parliament assembled.) This growth of industry during the last century, coupled with the reawakening of the whole Mediterranean, took form politically in the Catalan movement for secession from Spain, and in literature in the resurrection of Catalan thought and Catalan language.

Naturally the first generation was not interested in the manufactures that were the dynamo that generated the ferment of their lives. They had first to state the emotions of the mountains and the sea and of ancient heroic stories that had been bottled up in their race during centuries of inexpressiveness. For another generation perhaps the symbols will be the cluck of oiled cogs, the whirring of looms, the dragon forms of smoke spewed out of tall chimneys, and the substance will be the painful struggle for freedom, for sunnier, richer life of the huddled mobs of the slaves of the machines. For the first men conscious of their status as Catalans the striving was to make permanent their individual lives in terms of political liberty, of the mist-capped mountains and the changing sea.

Of this first generation was Juan Maragall who died in 1912, five years after the shooting of Ferrer, after a life spent almost entirely in Barcelona writing for newspapers,—as far as one can gather, a completely peaceful well-married existence, punctuated by a certain amount of political agitation in the cause of the independence of Catalonia, the life of a placid and recognized literary figure; *"un maître"* the French would have called him.

Perhaps six centuries before, in Palma de Mallorca, a young nobleman, a poet, a skilled player on the lute had stood tiptoe for attainment before the high-born and very stately lady he had courted through many moonlight nights, when her eye had chilled his quivering love suddenly and she had pulled open her bodice with both hands and shown him her breasts, one white and firm and the other swollen black and purple with cancer. The horror of the sight

of such beauty rotting away before his eyes had turned all his
passion inward and would have made him a saint had his ideas been
more orthodox; as it was the Blessed Ramón Lull lived to write
many mystical works in Catalan and Latin, in which he sought the
love of God in the love of Earth after the manner of the sufi of
Persia. Eventually he attained bloody martyrdom arguing with the
sages in some North African town. Somehow the spirit of the
tortured thirteenth-century mystic was born again in the calm
Barcelona journalist, whose life was untroubled by the impact of
events as could only be a life comprising the last half of the
nineteenth century. In Maragall's writings modulated in the lovely
homely language of the peasants and fishermen of Catalonia, there
flames again the passionate metaphor of Lull.

Here is a rough translation of one of his best known poems:

> At sunset time
> drinking at the spring's edge
> I drank down the secrets
> of mysterious earth.
>
> Deep in the runnel
> I saw the stainless water
> born out of darkness
> for the delight of my mouth,
>
> and it poured into my throat
> and with its clear spurting
> there filled me entirely
> mellowness of wisdom.
>
> When I stood straight and looked,
> mountains and woods and meadows
> seemed to me otherwise,
> everything altered.
>
> Above the great sunset
> there already shone through the glowing
> carmine contours of the clouds
> the white sliver of the new moon.
>
> It was a world in flower
> and the soul of it was I.
>
> I the fragrant soul of the meadows

that expands at flower-time and reaping-time.
I the peaceful soul of the herds
that tinkle half-hidden by the tall grass.
I the soul of the forest that sways in waves
like the sea, and has as far horizons.
And also I was the soul of the willow tree
that gives every spring its shade.
I the sheer soul of the cliffs
where the mist creeps up and scatters.
And the unquiet soul of the stream
that shrieks in shining waterfalls.
I was the blue soul of the pond
that looks with strange eyes on the wanderer.
I the soul of the all-moving wind
and the humble soul of opening flowers.
I was the height of the high peaks...
The clouds caressed me with great gestures
and the wide love of misty spaces
clove to me, placid.
I felt the delightfulness of springs
born in my flanks, gifts of the glaciers;
and in the ample quietude of horizons
I felt the reposeful sleep of storms.
And when the sky opened about me
and the sun laughed on my green planes
people, far off, stood still all day
staring at my sovereign beauty.
But I, full of the lust
that makes furious the sea and mountains
lifted myself up strongly through the sky
lifted the diversity of my flanks and entrails...
At sunset time
drinking at the spring's edge
I drank down the secrets
of mysterious earth.

The sea and mountains, mist and cattle and yellow broom-flowers,
and fishing boats with lateen sails like dark wings against the sunrise

towards Mallorca: delight of the nose and the eyes and the ears in all living perceptions until the poison of other-worldliness wells up suddenly in him and he is a Christian and a mystic full of echoes of old soul-torturing. In Maragall's most expressive work, a sequence of poems called *El Comte Arnau*, all this is synthesized. These are from the climax.

> All the voices of the earth
> acclaim count Arnold
> because from the dark trial
> he has come back triumphant.

> "Son of the earth, son of the earth,
> count Arnold,
> now ask, now ask
> what cannot you do?"

> "Live, live, live forever,
> I would never die:
> to be like a wheel revolving;
> to live with wine and a sword."

> "Wheels roll, roll,
> but they count the years."
> "Then I would be a rock
> immobile to suns or storms."

> "Rock lives without life
> forever impenetrable."

> "Then the ever-moving sea
> that opens a path for all things."

> "The sea is alone, alone,
> you go accompanied."

> "Then be the air when it flames
> in the light of the deathless sun."

> "But air and sun are loveless,
> ignorant of eternity."

> "Then to be man more than man
> to be earth palpitant."

> "You shall be wheel and rock,
> you shall be the mist-veiled sea
> you shall be the air in flame,

you shall be the whirling stars,
you shall be man more than man
for you have the will for it.
You shall run the plains and hills,
all the earth that is so wide,
mounted on a horse of flame
you shall be tireless, terrible
as the tramp of the storms
All the voices of earth
will cry out whirling about you.
They will call you spirit in torment
call you forever damned."

Night. All the beauty of Adalaisa
asleep at the feet of naked Christ.
Arnold goes pacing a dark path;
there is silence among the mountains;
in front of him the rustling lisp of a river,
a pool.... Then it is lost and soundless.
Arnold stands under the sheer portal.

He goes searching the cells for Adalaisa
and sees her sleeping, beautiful, prone
at the feet of the naked Christ, without veil
without kerchief, without cloak, gestureless,
without any defense, there, sleeping....
She had a great head of turbulent hair.

"How like fine silk your hair, Adalaisa,"
thinks Arnold. But he looks at her silently.
She sleeps, she sleeps and little by little
a flush spreads over all her face
as if a dream had crept through her gently
until she laughs aloud very softly
with a tremulous flutter of the lips.

"What amorous lips, Adalaisa,"
thinks Arnold. But he looks at her silently.

A great sigh swells through her, sleeping,
like a seawave, and fades to stillness.

"What sighs swell in your breast, Adalaisa,"
thinks Arnold. But he stares at her silently.

But when she opens her eyes he, awake,

tingling, carries her off in his arms.
When they burst out into the open fields
it is day.

But the fear of life gushes suddenly to muddy the dear wellspring
of sensation, and the poet, beaten to his knees, writes:

And when the terror-haunted moment comes
to close these earthly eyes of mine,
open for me, Lord, other greater eyes
to look upon the immensity of your face.

But before that moment comes, through the medium of an
extraordinarily terse and unspoiled language, a language that has not
lost its earthy freshness by mauling and softening at the hands of
literary generations, what a lilting crystal-bright vision of things. It is
as if the air of the Mediterranean itself, thin, brilliant, had been
hammered into cadences. The verse is leaping and free, full of
echoes and refrains. The images are sudden and unlabored like the
images in the Greek anthology: a hermit released from
Nebuchadnezzar's spell gets to his feet "like a bear standing
upright"; fishing boats being shoved off the beach slide into the sea
one by one "like village girls joining a dance"; on a rough day the
smacks with reefed sails "skip like goats at the harbor entrance."
There are phrases like "the great asleepness of the mountains"; "a
long sigh like a seawave through her sleep"; "my speech of her is
like a flight of birds that lead your glance into intense blue sky";
"the disquieting unquiet sea." Perhaps it is that the eyes are
sharpened by the yearning to stare through the brilliant changing
forms of things into some intenser beyond. Perhaps it takes a hot
intoxicating draught of divinity to melt into such white fire the
various colors of the senses. Perhaps earthly joy is intenser for the
beckoning flames of hell.

The daily life, too, to which Maragall aspires seems strangely out
of another age. That came home to me most strongly once, talking
to a Catalan after a mountain scramble in the eastern end of
Mallorca. We sat looking at the sea that was violet with sunset,

where the sails of the homecoming fishing boats were the wan yellow of primroses. Behind us the hills were sharp pyrites blue. From a window in the adobe hut at one side of us came a smell of sizzling olive oil and tomatoes and peppers and the muffled sound of eggs being beaten. We were footsore, hungry, and we talked about women and love. And after all it was marriage that counted, he told me at last, women's bodies and souls and the love of them were all very well, but it was the ordered life of a family, children, that counted; the family was the immortal chain on which lives were strung; and he recited this quatrain, saying, in that proud awefilled tone with which Latins speak of creative achievement, "By our greatest poet, Juan Maragall":

> Canta esposa, fila i canta
> que el patí em faras suau
> Quan l'esposa canta i fila
> el casal s'adorm en pau.

It was hard explaining how all our desires lay towards the completer and completer affirming of the individual, that we in Anglo-Saxon countries felt that the family was dead as a social unit, that new cohesions were in the making.

"I want my liberty," he broke in, "as much as—as Byron did, liberty of thought and action." He was silent a moment; then he said simply, "But I want a wife and children and a family, mine, mine."

Then the girl who was cooking leaned out of the window to tell us in soft Mallorquin that supper was ready. She had a full brown face flushed on the cheek-bones and given triangular shape like an El Greco madonna's face by the bright blue handkerchief knotted under the chin. Her breasts hung out from her body, solid like a Victory's under the sleek grey shawl as she leaned from the window. In her eyes that were sea-grey there was an unimaginable calm. I thought of Penelope sitting beside her loom in a smoky-raftered hall, grey eyes looking out on a sailless sea. And for a moment I understood the Catalan's phrase: the family was the chain on which lives were strung, and all of Maragall's lyricizing of wifehood,

> When the wife sits singing as she spins
> all the house can sleep in peace.

From the fishermen's huts down the beach came an intense blue smoke of fires; above the soft rustle of the swell among the boats came the chatter of many sleepy voices, like the sound of sparrows in a city park at dusk. The day dissolved slowly in utter timelessness. And when the last fishing boat came out of the dark sea, the tall slanting sail folding suddenly as the wings of a sea-gull alighting, the red-brown face of the man in the bow was the face of returning Odysseus. It was not the continuity of men's lives I felt, but their oneness. On that beach, beside that sea, there was no time.

When we were eating in the whitewashed room by the light of three brass olive oil lamps, I found that my argument had suddenly crumbled. What could I, who had come out of ragged and barbarous outlands, tell of the art of living to a man who had taught me both system and revolt? So am I, to whom the connubial lyrics of Patmore and Ella Wheeler Wilcox have always seemed inexpressible soiling of possible loveliness, forced to bow before the rich cadences with which Juan Maragall, Catalan, poet of the Mediterranean, celebrates the *familia*.

And in Maragall's work it is always the Mediterranean that one feels, the Mediterranean and the men who sailed on it in black ships with bright pointed sails. Just as in Homer and Euripides and Pindar and Theocritus and in that tantalizing kaleidoscope, the Anthology, beyond the grammar and the footnotes and the desolation of German texts there is always the rhythm of sea waves and the smell of well-caulked ships drawn up on dazzling beaches, so in Maragall, beyond the graceful well-kept literary existence, beyond wife and children and pompous demonstrations in the cause of abstract freedom, there is the sea lashing the rocky shins of the Pyrenees,—actual, dangerous, wet.

In this day when we Americans are plundering the earth far and near for flowers and seeds and ferments of literature in the hope, perhaps vain, of fallowing our thin soil with manure rich and diverse and promiscuous so that the somewhat sickly plants of our own culture may burst sappy and green through the steel and cement and inhibitions of our lives, we should not forget that northwest corner of the Mediterranean where the Langue d'Oc is as terse and salty as it was in the days of Pierre Vidal, whose rhythms of life, intrinsically Mediterranean, are finding new permanence—poetry richly ordered and lucid.

To the Catalans of the last fifty years has fallen the heritage of the oar which the cunning sailor Odysseus dedicated to the Sea, the earth-shaker, on his last voyage. And the first of them is Maragall.

XIII

On the top step Telemachus found a man sitting with his head in his hands moaning *"¡Ay de mí!"* over and over again.

"I beg pardon," he said stiffly, trying to slip by.

"Did you see the function this evening, sir?" asked the man looking up at Telemachus with tears streaming from his eyes. He had a yellow face with lean blue chin and jowls shaven close and a little waxed moustache that had lost all its swagger for the moment as he had the ends of it in his mouth.

"What function?"

"In the theatre…. I am an artist, an actor." He got to his feet and tried to twirl his ragged moustaches back into shape. Then he stuck out his chest, straightened his waistcoat so that the large watchchain clinked, and invited Telemachus to have a cup of coffee with him.

They sat at the black oak table in front of the fire. The actor told how there had been only twelve people at his show. How was he to be expected to make his living if only twelve people came to see him? And the night before Carnival, too, when they usually got such a crowd. He'd learned a new song especially for the occasion, too good, too artistic for these pigs of provincials.

"Here in Spain the stage is ruined, ruined!" he cried out finally.

"How ruined?" asked Telemachus.

"The *Zarzuela* is dead. The days of the great writers of *zarzuela* have gone never to return. O the music, the lightness, the jollity of the *zarzuela*s of my father's time! My father was a great singer, a tenor whose voice was an enchantment…. I know the princely life of a great singer of *zarzuela*…. When a small boy I lived it…. And now look at me!"

Telemachus thought how strangely out of place was the actor's anæmic wasplike figure in this huge kitchen where everything was dark, strong-smelling, massive. Black beams with here and there a trace of red daub on them held up the ceiling and bristled with square iron spikes from which hung hams and sausages and white strands of garlic. The table at which they sat was an oak slab, black from smoke and generations of spillings, firmly straddled on thick trestles. Over the fire hung a copper pot, sooty, with a glitter of grease on it where the soup had boiled over. When one leaned to put a bundle of sticks on the fire one could see up the chimney an oblong patch of blackness spangled with stars. On the edge of the hearth was the great hunched figure of the *padrón*, half asleep, a silk handkerchief round his head, watching the coffee-pot.

"It was an elegant life, full of voyages," went on the actor. "South America, Naples, Sicily, and all over Spain. There were formal dinners, receptions, ceremonial dress.... Ladies of high society came to congratulate us.... I played all the child rôles.... When I was fourteen a duchess fell in love with me. And now, look at me, ragged, dying of hunger—not even able to fill a theatre in this hog of a village. In Spain they have lost all love of the art. All they want is foreign importations, Viennese musical comedies, smutty farces from Paris...."

"With cognac or rum?" the *padrón* roared out suddenly in his deep voice, swinging the coffee pot up out of the fire.

"Cognac," said the actor. "What rotten coffee!" He gave little petulant sniffs as he poured sugar into his glass.

The wail of a baby rose up suddenly out of the dark end of the kitchen.

The actor took two handfuls of his hair and yanked at them.

"Ay my nerves!" he shrieked. The baby wailed louder in spasm after spasm of yelling. The actor jumped to his feet, "¡Dolóres, Dolóres, *ven acá!*"

After he had called several times a girl came into the room padding softly on bare feet and stood before him tottering sleepily in the firelight. Her heavy lids hung over her eyes. A strand of black hair curled round her full throat and spread raggedly over her breasts. She had pulled a blanket over her shoulders but through a rent in her coarse nightgown the fire threw a patch of red glow curved like a rose petal about one brown thigh.

"*¡Qué desvergonza'a!*... How shameless!" muttered the *padrón*.

The actor was scolding her in a shrill endless whine. The girl stood still without answering, her teeth clenched to keep them from chattering. Then she turned without a word and brought the baby from the packing box in which he lay at the end of the room, and drawing the blanket about both her and the child crouched on her heels very close to the flame with her bare feet in the ashes. When the crying had ceased she turned to the actor with a full-lipped smile and said, "There's nothing the matter with him, Paco. He's not even hungry. You woke him up, the poor little angel, talking so loud."

She got to her feet again, and with slow unspeakable dignity walked back and forth across the end of the room with the child at her breast. Each time she turned she swung the trailing blanket round with a sudden twist of her body from the hips.

Telemachus watched her furtively, sniffing the hot aroma of coffee and cognac from his glass, and whenever she turned the muscles of his body drew into tight knots from joy.

"*Es buena chica*.... She's a nice kid, from Malaga. I picked her up there. A little stupid.... But these days...." the actor was saying with much shrugging of the shoulders. "She dances well, but the public doesn't like her. *No tiene cara de parisiana.* She hasn't the Parisian air.... But these days, *vamos*, one can't be too fastidious. This taste for French plays, French women, French cuisine, it's ruined the Spanish theatre."

The fire flared crackling. Telemachus sat sipping his coffee waiting for the unbearable delight of the swing of the girl's body as she turned to pace back towards him across the room.

XIV

All the gravel paths of the Plaza Santa Ana were encumbered with wicker chairs. At one corner seven blind musicians all in a row, with violins, a cello, guitars and a mournful cornet, toodled and wheezed and twiddled through the "Blue Danube." At another a crumpled old man, with a monkey dressed in red silk drawers on his shoulder, ground out "*la Paloma*" from a hurdygurdy. In the middle of the green plot a fountain sparkled in the yellow light that streamed horizontally from the cafés fuming with tobacco smoke on two sides of the square, and ragged guttersnipes dipped their legs in the slimy basin round about it, splashing one another, rolling like little colts in the grass. From the cafés and the wicker chairs and tables, clink of glasses and dominoes, patter of voices, scuttle of waiters with laden trays, shouts of men selling shrimps, prawns, fried potatoes, watermelon, nuts in little cornucopias of red, green, or yellow paper. Light gleamed on the buff-colored disk of a table in front of me, on the rims of two beer-mugs, in the eyes of a bearded man with an aquiline nose very slender at the bridge who leaned towards me talking in a deep even voice, telling me in swift lisping Castilian stories of Madrid. First of the Madrid of Felipe Cuarto: *corridas* in the Plaza Mayor, *auto da fé*, pictures by Velasquez on view under the arcade where now there is a doughnut and coffee shop, pompous coaches painted vermilion, cobalt, gilded, stuffed with ladies in vast bulge of damask and brocade, plumed cavaliers, pert ogling pages, lurching and swaying through the foot-deep stinking mud of the streets; plays of Calderon and Lope presented in gardens tinkling with jewels and sword-chains where ladies of the court flirted behind ostrich fans with stiff lean-faced lovers. Then

Goya's Madrid: riots in the Puerta del Sol, *majas* leaning from balconies, the fair of San Isidro by the river, scuttling of ragged guerrilla bands, brigands and patriots; tramp of the stiffnecked grenadiers of Napoleon; pompous little men in short-tailed wigs dying the *dos de Mayo* with phrases from Mirabeau on their lips under the brick arch of the arsenal; frantic carnivals of the Burial of the Sardine; naked backs of flagellants dripping blood, lovers hiding under the hoop skirts of the queen. Then the romantic Madrid of the thirties, Larra, Becquer, Espronceda, Byronic gestures, vigils in graveyards, duels, struttings among the box-alleys of the Retiro, pale young men in white stocks shooting themselves in attics along the Calle Mayor. "And now," the voice became suddenly gruff with anger, "look at Madrid. They closed the Café Suizo, they are building a subway, the Castellana looks more like the Champs Elysées every day…. It's only on the stage that you get any remnant of the real Madrid. Benavente is the last *madrileño. Tiene el sentido de lo castizo.* He has the sense of the …" all the end of the evening went to the discussion of the meaning of the famous word "*castizo.*"

The very existence of such a word in a language argues an acute sense of style, of the manner of doing things. Like all words of real import its meaning is a gamut, a section of a spectrum rather than something fixed and irrevocable. The first implication seems to be "according to Hoyle," following tradition: a neatly turned phrase, an essentially Castilian cadence, is *castizo*; a piece of pastry or a poem in the old tradition are *castizo*, or a compliment daintily turned, or a cloak of the proper fullness with the proper red velvet-bordered lining gracefully flung about the ears outside of a café. *Lo castizo* is the essence of the local, of the regional, the last stronghold of Castilian arrogance, refers not to the empty shell of traditional observances but to the very core and gesture of them. Ultimately *lo castizo* means all that is salty, savourous of the red and yellow hills and the bare plains and the deep *arroyos* and the dust-colored towns full of palaces and belfries, and the beggars in snuff-colored cloaks and the mule-drivers with blankets over their shoulders, and the discursive lean-faced gentlemen grouped about tables at cafés and casinos, and the stout dowagers with mantillas over their gleaming black hair walking to church in the morning with missals clasped in fat hands, all that is acutely indigenous, Iberian, in the life of Castile.

In the flood of industrialism that for the last twenty years has swelled to obliterate landmarks, to bring all the world to the same level of nickel-plated dullness, the theatre in Madrid has been the refuge of *lo castizo*. It has been a theatre of manners and local types and customs, of observation and natural history, where a rather specialized well-trained audience accustomed to satire as the tone of daily conversation was tickled by any portrayal of its quips and cranks. A tradition of character-acting grew up nearer that of the Yiddish theatre than of any other stage we know in America. Benavente and the brothers Quintero have been the playwrights who most typified the school that has been in vogue since the going out of the *drame passionel* style of Echegaray. At present Benavente as director of the *Teatro Nacional* is unquestionably the leading figure. Therefore it is very fitting that Benavente should be in life and works of all *madrileños* the most *castizo*.

Later, as we sat drinking milk in la Granja after a couple of hours of a shabby third-generation Viennese musical show at the Apollo, my friend discoursed to me of the manner of life of the *madrileño* in general and of Don Jacinto Benavente in particular. Round eleven or twelve one got up, took a cup of thick chocolate, strolled on the Castellana under the chestnut trees or looked in at one's office in the theatre. At two one lunched. At three or so one sat a while drinking coffee or anis in the Gato Negro, where the waiters have the air of cabinet ministers and listen to every word of the rather languid discussions on art and letters that while away the afternoon hours. Then as it got towards five one drifted to a matinee, if there chanced to be a new play opening, or to tea somewhere out in the new Frenchified Barrio de Salamanca. Dinner came along round nine; from there one went straight to the theatre to see that all went

well with the evening performance. At one the day culminated in a
famous *tertulia* at the Café de Lisboa, where all the world met and
argued and quarreled and listened to disquisitions and epigrams at
tables stacked with coffee glasses amid spiral reek of cigarette
smoke.

"But when were the plays written?" I asked.

My friend laughed. "Oh between semicolons," he said, "and *en
route*, and in bed, and while being shaved. Here in Madrid you write
a comedy between biscuits at breakfast…. And now that the
Metro's open, it's a great help. I know a young poet who tossed off
a five-act tragedy, sex-psychology and all, between the Puerta del Sol
and Cuatro Caminos!"

"But Madrid's being spoiled," he went on sadly, "at least from the
point of view of *lo castizo*. In the last generation all one saw of
daylight were sunset and dawn, people used to go out to fight duels
where the Residencia de Estudiantes is now, and they had real
tertulias, tertulias where conversation swaggered and parried and
lunged, sparing nothing, laughing at everything, for all the world like
our unique Spanish hero, Don Juan Tenorio.

'Yo a las cabañas baje,
yo a los palacios subí,
y los claustros escalé,
y en todas partes dejé
memorias amargas de mí.'

"Talk ranged from peasant huts to the palaces of Carlist
duchesses, and God knows the crows and the cloisters weren't let
off scot free. And like good old absurd Tenorio they didn't care if
laughter did leave bitter memories, and were willing to wait till their
deathbeds to reconcile themselves with heaven and solemnity. But
our generation, they all went solemn in their cradles…. Except for
the theatre people, always except for the theatre people! We of the
theatres will be *castizo* to the death."

As we left the café, I to go home to bed, my friend to go on to
another *tertulia*, he stood for a moment looking back among the
tables and glasses.

"What the Agora was to the Athenians," he said, and finished the sentence with an expressive wave of the hand.

It's hard for Anglo-Saxons, ante-social, as suspicious of neighbors as if they still lived in the boggy forests of Finland, city-dwellers for a paltry thirty generations, to understand the publicity, the communal quality of life in the region of the Mediterranean. The first thought when one gets up is to go out of doors to see what people are talking of, the last thing before going to bed is to chat with the neighbors about the events of the day. The home, cloistered off, exclusive, can hardly be said to exist. Instead of the nordic hearth there is the courtyard about which the women sit while the men are away at the marketplace. In Spain this social life centers in the café and the casino. The modern theatre is as directly the offshoot of the café as the old theatre was of the marketplace where people gathered in front of the church porch to see an interlude or mystery acted by travelling players in a wagon. The people who write the plays, the people who act them and the people who see them spend their spare time smoking about marbletop tables, drinking coffee, discussing. Those too poor to buy a drink stand outside in groups on the sunny side of squares. Constant talk about everything that may happen or had happened or will happen manages to butter the bread of life pretty evenly with passion and thought and significance, but one loses the chunks of intensity. There is little chance for the burst dams that suddenly flood the dry watercourse of emotion among more inhibited, less civilized people. Generations upon generations of townsmen have made of life a well-dredged canal, easy-flowing, somewhat shallow.

It follows that the theatre under such conditions shall be talkative, witty, full of neat swift caricaturing, improvised, unselfconscious; at its worst, glib. Boisterous action often, passionate strain almost never. In Echegaray there are hecatombs, half the characters habitually go insane in the last act; tremendous barking but no bite of real intensity. Benavente has recaptured some of Lope de Vega's marvellous quality of adventurous progression. The Quinteros write domestic comedies full of whim and sparkle and tenderness. But expression always seems too easy; there is never the unbearable tension, the utter self-forgetfulness of the greatest drama. The Spanish theatre plays on the nerves and intellect rather than on the great harpstrings of emotion in which all of life is drawn taut.

At present in Madrid even café life is receding before the exigencies of business and the hardly excusable mania for imitating English and American manners. Spain is undergoing great changes in its relation to the rest of Europe, to Latin America, in its own internal structure. Notwithstanding Madrid's wartime growth and prosperity, the city is fast losing ground as the nucleus of the life and thought of Spanish-speaking people. The *madrileño*, lean, cynical, unscrupulous, nocturnal, explosive with a curious sort of febrile wit is becoming extinct. His theatre is beginning to pander to foreign tastes, to be ashamed of itself, to take on respectability and stodginess. Prices of seats, up to 1918 very low, rise continually; the artisans, apprentice boys, loafers, clerks, porters, who formed the backbone of the audiences can no longer afford the theatre and have taken to the movies instead. Managers spend money on scenery and costumes as a way of attracting fashionables. It has become quite proper for women to go to the theatre. Benavente's plays thus acquire double significance as the summing up and the chief expression of a movement that has reached its hey-day, from which the sap has already been cut off. It is, indeed, the thing to disparage them for their very finest quality, the vividness with which they express the texture of Madrid, the animated humorous mordant conversation about café tables: *lo castizo*.

The first play of his I ever saw, "*Gente Conocida*," impressed me, I remember, at a time when I understood about one word in ten and had to content myself with following the general modulation of things, as carrying on to the stage, the moment the curtain rose, the very people, intonations, phrases, that were stirring in the seats about me. After the first act a broad-bosomed lady in black silk leaned back in the seat beside me sighing comfortably "*Qué castizo es este Benavente*," and then went into a volley of approving chirpings. The full import of her enthusiasm did not come to me until much later when I read the play in the comparative light of a surer knowledge of Castilian, and found that it was a most vitriolic dissecting of the manner of life of that very dowager's own circle, a showing up of the predatory spite of "people of consequence." Here was this society woman, who in any other country would have been indignant, enjoying the annihilation of her kind. On such willingness to play the game of wit, even of abuse, without too much rancor, which is the unction to ease of social intercourse, is founded all the popularity of Benavente's writing. Somewhere in Hugo's Spanish grammar (God save the mark!) is a proverb to the effect that the wind of Madrid is so subtle that it will kill a man without putting out a candle. The same, at their best, can be said of Benavente's satiric comedies:

> El viento de Madrid es tan sutil
> que mata a un hombre y no apaga un candil.

From the opposite bank of the Manzanares, a slimy shrunken stream usually that flows almost hidden under clothes lines where billow the undergarments of all Madrid, in certain lights you can recapture almost entire the silhouette of the city as Goya has drawn it again and again; clots of peeling stucco houses huddling up a flattened hill towards the dome of San Francisco El Grande, then an undulating skyline with cupolas and baroque belfries jutting among the sudden lights and darks of the clouds. Then perhaps the sun will light up with a spreading shaft of light the electric-light factory, the sign on a biscuit manufacturer's warehouse, a row of white blocks of apartments along the edge of town to the north, and instead of odd grimy aboriginal Madrid, it will be a type city in Europe in the industrial era that shines in the sun beyond the blue shadows and creamy flashes of the clothes on the lines. So will it be in a few years with modernized Madrid, with the life of cafés and *paseos* and theatres. There will be moments when in American automats, elegant smokeless tearooms, shiny restaurants built in copy of those of Buenos Aires, someone who has read his Benavente will be able to catch momentary glimpses of old intonations, of witty parries, of noisy bombastic harangues and feel for one pentecostal moment the full and by that time forgotten import of *lo castizo*.

TALK BY THE ROAD

XV

The sun next morning was tingling warm. Telemachus strode along with a taste of a milky bowl of coffee and crisp *churros* in his mouth and a fresh wind in his hair; his feet rasped pleasantly on the gravel of the road. Behind him the town sank into the dun emerald-striped plain, roofs clustering, huddling more and more under the shadow of the beetling church, and the tower becoming leaner and darker against the steamy clouds that oozed in billowing tiers over the mountains to the north. Crows flapped about the fields where here and there the dark figures of a man and a pair of mules moved up a long slope. On the telegraph wires at a bend in the road two magpies sat, the sunlight glinting, when they stirred, on the white patches on their wings. Telemachus felt well-rested and content with himself.

"After all mother knows best," he was thinking. "That foolish Lyaeus will come dragging himself into Toledo a week from now."

Before noon he came on the same Don Alonso he had seen the day before in Illescas. Don Alonso was stretched out under an olive tree, a long red sausage in his hand, a loaf of bread and a small leather bottle of wine on the sward in front of him. Hitched to the tree, at the bark of which he nibbled with long teeth, was the grey horse.

"*Hola*, my friend," cried Don Alonso, "still bent on Toledo?"

"How soon can I get there?"

"Soon enough to see the castle of San Servando against the sunset. We will go together. You travel as fast as my old nag. But do me the honor of eating something, you must be hungry." Thereupon Don Alonso handed Telemachus the sausage and a knife to peel and slice it with.

"How early you must have started."

They sat together munching bread and sausage to which the sweet pepper mashed into it gave a bright red color, and occasionally, head thrown back, let a little wine squirt into their mouths from the bottle.

Don Alonso waved discursively a bit of sausage held between bread by tips of long grey fingers.

"You are now, my friend, in the heart of Castile. Look, nothing but live-oaks along the gulches and wheat-lands rolling up under a tremendous sky. Have you ever seen more sky? In Madrid there is not so much sky, is there? In your country there is not so much sky? Look at the huge volutes of those clouds. This is a setting for thoughts as mighty in contour as the white cumulus over the Sierra, such as come into the minds of men lean, wind-tanned, long-striding...." Don Alonso put a finger to his high yellow forehead. "There is in Castile a potential beauty, my friend, something humane, tolerant, vivid, robust.... I don't say it is in me. My only merit lies in recognizing it, formulating it, for I am no more than a thinker.... But the day will come when in this gruff land we shall have flower and fruit."

Don Alonso was smiling with thin lips, head thrown back against the twisted trunk of the olive tree. Then all at once he got to his feet, and after rummaging a moment in the little knapsack that hung over his shoulder, produced absent-mindedly a handful of small white candies the shape of millstones which he stared at in a puzzled way for some seconds.

"After all," he went on, "they make famous sweets in these old Castilian towns. These are *melindres*. Have one.... When people, d'you know, are kind to children, there are things to be expected."

"Certainly children are indulgently treated in Spain," said Telemachus, his mouth full of almond paste. "They actually seem to like children!"

A cart drawn by four mules tandem led by a very minute donkey with three strings of blue beads round his neck was jingling past along the road. As the canvas curtains of the cover were closed the only evidence of the driver was a sleepy song in monotone that trailed with the dust cloud after the cart. While they stood by the roadside watching the joggle of it away from them down the road, a flushed face was poked out from between the curtains and a voice cried "Hello, Tell"

"It's Lyaeus," cried Telemachus and ran after the cart bubbling with curiosity to hear his companion's adventures.

With a angle of mulebells and a hoarse shout from the driver the cart stopped, and Lyaeus tumbled out. His hair was mussed and there were wisps of hay on his clothes. He immediately stuck his head back in through the curtains. By the time Telemachus reached him the cart was tinkling its way down the road again and Lyaeus stood grinning, blinking sleepy eyes in the middle of the road, in one hand a skin of wine, in the other a canvas bag.

"What ho!" cried Telemachus.

"Figs and wine," said Lyaeus. Then, as Don Alonso came up leading his grey horse, he added in an explanatory tone, "I was asleep in the cart."

"Well?" said Telemachus.

"O it's such a long story," said Lyaeus.

Walking beside them, Don Alonso was reciting into his horse's ear:

'Sigue la vana sombra, el bien fingido.
El hombre está entregado
al sueño, de su suerte no cuidando,
y con paso callado
el cielo vueltas dando
las horas del vivir le va hurtando.'

"Whose is that?" said Lyaeus.

"The revolving sky goes stealing his hours of life…. But I don't know," said Don Alonso, "perhaps like you, this Spain of ours makes ground sleeping as well as awake. What does a day matter? The driver snores but the good mules jog on down the appointed road."

Then without another word he jumped on his horse and with a smile and a wave of the hand trotted off ahead of them.

XVI

Doce días son pasados
después que el Cid acabára
aderézanse las gentes
para salir a batalla
con Búcar ese rey moro
y contra la su canalla.
Cuando fuera media noche
el cuerpo así coma estaba
le ponen sobre Babieca
y al caballo lo ataban.

I

And when the army sailed out of Valencia the Moors of King Bucar fled before the dead body of the Cid and ten thousand of them were drowned trying to scramble into their ships, among them twenty kings, and the Christians got so much booty of gold and silver among the tents that the poorest of them became a rich man. Then the army continued, the dead Cid riding each day's journey on his horse, across the dry mountains to Sant Pedro de Cardeña in Castile where the king Don Alfonso had come from Toledo, and he seeing the Cid's face still so beautiful and his beard so long and his eyes so flaming ordered that instead of closing the body in a coffin with gold nails they should set it upright in a chair beside the altar, with the sword Tizona in its hand. And there the Cid stayed more than ten years.

Mandó que no se enterrase
sino que el cuerpo arreado
se ponga junto al altar
y a Tizona en la su mano;

In the pass above people were skiing. On the hard snow of the road there were orange-skins. A victoria had just driven by in which sat a bored inflated couple much swathed in furs.

"Where on earth are they going?"

"To the Puerta de Navecerrada," my friend answered.

"But they look as if they'd be happier having tea at Molinero's than paddling about up there in the snow."

"They would be, but it's the style… winter sports… and all because a lithe little brown man who died two years ago liked the mountains. Before him no *madrileño* ever knew the Sierra existed."

"Who was that?"

"Don Francisco Giner."

That afternoon when it was already getting dark we were scrambling wet, chilled, our faces lashed by the snow, down through drifts from a shoulder of Siete Picos with the mist all about us and nothing but the track of a flock of sheep for a guide. The light from a hut pushed a long gleaming orange finger up the mountainside. Once inside we pulled off our shoes and stockings and toasted our feet at a great fireplace round which were flushed faces, glint of teeth in laughter, schoolboys and people from the university shouting and declaiming, a smell of tea and wet woolens. Everybody was noisy with the rather hysterical excitement that warmth brings after exertion in cold mountain air. Cheeks were purple and tingling. A young man with fuzzy yellow hair told me a story in French about the Emperor of Morocco, and produced a tin of potted blackbirds which it came out were from the said personage's private stores. Unending fountains of tea seethed in two smoke-blackened pots on the hearth. In the back of the hut among leaping shadows were piles of skis and the door, which occasionally opened to let in a new wet snowy figure and shut again on skimming snow-gusts. Everyone was rocked with enormous jollity. Train time came suddenly and we ran and stumbled and slid the miles to the station through the dark, down the rocky path.

In the third-class carriage people sang songs as the train jounced its way towards the plain and Madrid. The man who sat next to me asked me if I knew it was Don Francisco who had had that hut built for the children of the Institución Libre de Inseñanza. Little by little he told me the history of the Krausistas and Francisco Giner de los Ríos and the revolution of 1873, a story like enough to many others in the annals of the nineteenth century movement for education, but in its overtones so intimately Spanish and individual that it came as the explanation of many things I had been wondering about and gave me an inkling of some of the origins of a rather special mentality I had noticed in people I knew about Madrid.

Somewhere in the forties a professor of the Universidad Central, Sanz del Río, was sent to Germany to study philosophy on a government scholarship. Spain was still in the intellectual coma that had followed the failure of the Cortes of Cadiz and the restoration of Fernando Septimo. A decade or more before, Larra, the last flame of romantic revolt, had shot himself for love in Madrid. In Germany, at Heidelberg, Sanz del Río found dying Krause, the first archpriest who stood interpreting between Kant and the world. When he returned to Spain he refused to take up his chair at the university saying he must have time to think out his problems, and retired to a tiny room—a room so dark that they say that to read he had to sit on a stepladder under the window in the town of Illescas, where was another student, Greco's San Ildefonso. There he lived several years in seclusion. When he did return to the university it was to refuse to make the profession of political and religious faith required by a certain prime minister named Orovio. He was dismissed and several of his disciples. At the same time Francisco Giner de los Ríos, then a young man who had just gained an appointment with great difficulty because of his liberal ideas, resigned out of solidarity with the rest. In 1868 came the liberal revolution which was the political expression of this whole movement, and all these professors were reinstated. Until the restoration of the Bourbons in '75 Spain was a hive of modernization, Europeanization.

Returned to power Orovio lost no time in republishing his decrees of a profession of faith. Giner, Ascárate, Salmerón and several others were arrested and exiled to distant fortresses when they protested; their friends declared themselves in sympathy and lost their jobs, and many other professors resigned, so that the university was at one blow denuded of its best men. From this came the idea of founding a free university which should be supported entirely by private subscription. From that moment the life of Giner de los Ríos was completely entwined with the growth of the Institución Libre de Inseñanza, which developed in the course of a few years into a coeducational primary school. And directly or indirectly there is not a single outstanding figure in Spanish life today whose development was not largely influenced by this dark slender baldheaded old man with a white beard whose picture one finds on people's writing desks.

> ... Oh, sí, llevad, amigos,
> su cuerpo a la montaña
> a los azules montes
> del ancho Guadarrama,

wrote his pupil, Antonio Machado—and I rather think Machado is the pupil whose name will live the longest—after Don Francisco's death in 1915.

> ... Yes, carry, friends
> his body to the hills
> to the blue peaks
> of the wide Guadarrama.
> There are deep gulches
> of green pines where the wind sings.
> There is rest for his spirit
> under a cold live oak
> in loam full of thyme, where play
> golden butterflies....
> There the master one day
> dreamed new flowerings for Spain.

These are fragments from an elegy by Juan Ramon Jiménez, another poet-pupil of Don Francisco:

"Don Francisco.... It seemed that he summed up all that is tender and keen in life: flowers, flames, birds, peaks, children.... Now, stretched on his bed, like a frozen river that perhaps still flows under the ice, he is the clear path for endless recurrence.... He was like a living statue of himself, a statue of earth, of wind, of water, of fire. He had so freed himself from the husk of every day that talking to him we might have thought we were talking to his image. Yes. One would have said he wasn't going to die: that he had already passed, without anybody's knowing it, beyond death; that he was with us forever, like a spirit.

"In the little door of the bedroom one already feels well-being. A trail of the smell of thyme and violets that comes and goes with the breeze from the open window leads like a delicate hand towards where he lies.... Peace. All death has done has been to infuse the color of his skin with a deep violet veiling of ashes.

"What a suave smell, and how excellent death is here! No rasping essences, none of the exterior of blackness and crêpe. All this is white and uncluttered, like a hut in the fields in Andalusia, like the whitewashed portal of some garden in the south. All just as it was. Only he who was there has gone."

"The day is fading, with a little wind that has a premonition of spring. In the window panes is a confused mirroring of rosy clouds. The blackbird, the blackbird that he must have heard for thirty years, that he'd have liked to have gone on hearing dead, has come to see if he's listening. Peace. The bedroom and the garden strive quietly light against light: the brightness of the bedroom is stronger and glows out into the afternoon. A sparrow flutters up into the sudden stain with which the sun splashes the top of a tree and sits there twittering. In the shadow below the blackbird whistles once more. Now and then one seems to hear the voice that is silenced forever."

"How pleasant to be here! It's like sitting beside a spring, reading under a tree, like letting the stream of a lyric river carry one away.... And one feels like never moving: like plucking to infinity, as one might tear roses to pieces, these white full hours; like clinging forever to this clear teacher in the eternal twilight of this last lesson of austerity and beauty."

"'Municipal Cemetery' it says on the gate, so that one may know, opposite that other sign 'Catholic Cemetery,' so that one may also know."

"He didn't want to be buried in that cemetery, so opposed to the smiling savourous poetry of his spirit. But it had to be. He'll still hear the blackbirds of the familiar garden. 'After all,' says Cossio, 'I don't think he'll be sorry to spend a little while with Don Julián....'"

"Careful hands have taken the dampness out of the earth with thyme; on the coffin they have thrown roses, narcissus, violets. There comes, lost, an aroma of last evening, a bit of the bedroom from which they took so much away...."

"Silence. Faint sunlight. Great piles of cloud full of wind drag frozen shadows across us, and through them flying low, black grackles. In the distance Guadarrama, chaste beyond belief, lifts crystals of cubed white light. Some tiny bird trills for a second in the sown fields nearby that are already vaguely greenish, then lights on the creamy top of a tomb, then flies away...."

"Neither impatience nor cares; slowness and forgetfulness.... Silence. In the silence, the voice of a child walking through the fields, the sound of a sob hidden among the tombstones, the wind, the broad wind of these days...."

"I've seen occasionally a fire put out with earth. Innumerable little tongues spurted from every side. A pupil of his who was a mason made for this extinguished fire its palace of mud on a piece of earth two friends kept free. He has at the head a euonymus, young and strong, and at the foot, already full of sprouts with coming spring, an acacia…."

Round El Pardo the evergreen oaks, encinas, are scattered sparsely, tight round heads of blue green, over hills that in summer are yellow like the haunches of lions. From Madrid to El Pardo was one of Don Francisco's favorite walks, out past the jail, where over the gate is written an echo of his teaching: "Abhor the crime but pity the criminal," past the palace of Moncloa with its stately abandoned gardens, and out along the Manzanares by a road through the royal domain where are gamekeepers with shotguns and signs of "Beware the mantraps," then up a low hill from which one sees the Sierra Guadarrama piled up against the sky to the north, greenish snow-peaks above long blue foothills and all the foreground rolling land full of clumps of encinas, and at last into the little village with its barracks and its dilapidated convent and its planetrees in front of the mansion Charles V built. It was under an encina that I sat all one long morning reading up in reviews and textbooks on the theory of law, the life and opinions of Don Francisco. In the moments when the sun shone the heat made the sticky cistus bushes with the glistening white flowers all about me reek with pungence. Then a cool whisp of wind would bring a chill of snow-slopes from the mountains and a passionless indefinite fragrance of distances. At intervals a church bell would toll in a peevish importunate manner from the boxlike convent on the hill opposite. I was reading an account of the philosophical concept of monism, cudgelling my brain with phrases. And his fervent love of nature made the master evoke occasionally in class this beautiful image of the great poet and philosopher Schelling: "Man is the eye with which the spirit of nature contemplates itself"; and then having qualified with a phrase Schelling's expression, he would turn on those who see in nature manifestation of the rough, the gross, the instinctive, and offer for meditation this saying of Michelet: "Cloth woven by a weaver is just as natural as that a spider weaves. All is in one Being, all is in the Idea and for the Idea, the latter being understood in the way Platonic substantialism has been interpreted...."

In the grass under my book were bright fronds of moss, among which very small red ants performed prodigies of mountaineering, while along tramped tunnels long black ants scuttled darkly, glinting when the light struck them. The smell of cistus was intense, hot, full of spices as the narrow streets of an oriental town at night. In the distance the mountains piled up in zones olive green, Prussian blue, ultra-marine, white. A cold wind-gust turned the pages of the book. Thought and passion, reflection and instinct, affections, emotions, impulses collaborate in the rule of custom, which is revealed not in words declared and promulgated in view of future conduct, but in the act itself, tacit, taken for granted, or, according to the energetic expression of the Digest: *rebus et factis*. Over "factis," sat a little green and purple fly with the body curved under at the table. I wondered vaguely if it was a Mayfly. And then all of a sudden it was clear to me that these books, these dusty philosophical phrases, these mortuary articles by official personages were dimming the legend in my mind, taking the brilliance out of the indirect but extraordinarily personal impact of the man himself. They embalmed the Cid and set him up in the church with his sword in his hand, for all men to see. What sort of legend would a technical disquisition by the archbishop on his theory of the angle of machicolations have generated in men's minds? And what can a saint or a soldier or a founder of institutions leave behind him but a legend? Certainly it is not for the Franciscans that one remembers Francis of Assisi.

And the curious thing about the legend of a personality is that it may reach the highest fervor without being formulated. It is something by itself that stands behind anecdotes, death-notices, elegies.

In Madrid at the funeral of another of the great figures of nineteenth century Spain, Pérez Galdós, I stood on the curb beside a large-mouthed youth with a flattened toadlike face, who was balancing a great white-metal jar of milk on his shoulder. The plumed hearse and the carriages full of flowers had just passed. The street in front of us was a slow stream of people very silent, their feet shuffling, shuffling, feet in patent-leather shoes and spats, feet in square-toed shoes, pointed-toed shoes, *alpargatas*, canvas sandals; people along the sides seemed unable to resist the suction of it, joined in unostentatiously to follow if only a few moments the procession of the legend of Don Benito. The boy with the milk turned to me and said how lucky it was they were burying Galdós, he'd have an excuse for being late for the milk. Then suddenly he pulled his cap off and became enormously excited and began offering cigarettes to everyone round about. He scratched his head and said in the voice of a Saul stricken on the road to Damascus: "How many books he must have written, that gentleman! *¡Cáspita!*... It makes a fellow sorry when a gentleman like that dies," and shouldering his pail, his blue tunic fluttering in the wind, he joined the procession.

Like the milk boy I found myself joining the procession of the legend of Giner de los Ríos. That morning under the encina I closed up the volumes on the theory of law and the bulletins with their death-notices and got to my feet and looked over the tawny hills of El Bardo and thought of the little lithe baldheaded man with a white beard like the beard in El Greco's portrait of Covarrubias, who had taught a generation to love the tremendous contours of their country, to climb mountains and bathe in cold torrents, who was the first, it almost seems, to feel the tragic beauty of Toledo, who in a lifetime of courageous unobtrusive work managed to stamp all the men and women whose lives remotely touched his with the seal of his personality. Born in Ronda in the wildest part of Andalusia of a family that came from Vélez-Málaga, a white town near the sea in the rich fringes of the Sierra Nevada, he had the mental agility and the sceptical tolerance and the uproarious good nature of the people of that region, the sobriety and sinewiness of a mountaineer. His puritanism became a definite part of the creed of the hopeful discontented generations that are gradually, for better or for worse, remoulding Spain. His nostalgia of the north, of fjords where fir trees hang over black tidal waters, of blonde people cheerfully orderly in rectangular blue-tiled towns, became the gospel of Europeanization, of wholesale destruction of all that was individual, savage, African in the Spanish tradition. *Rebus et factis*. And yet none of the things and acts do much to explain the peculiar radiance of his memory, the jovial tenderness with which people tell one about him. The immanence of the man is such that even an outsider, one who like the milk boy at the funeral of Galdós meets the procession accidentally with another errand in his head, is drawn in almost without knowing it. It's impossible to think of him buried in a box in unconsecrated ground in the Cementerio Civil. In Madrid, in the little garden of the Institución where he used to teach the children, in front of a certain open fire in a certain house at El Pardo where they say he loved to sit and talk, I used to half expect to meet him, that some friend would take me to see him as they took people to see Cid in San Pedro de Cardeña.

> Cara tiene de hermosura
> muy hermosa y colorada;
> los ojos igual abiertos
> muy apuesta la su barba
> Non parece que está muerto
> antes vivo semejaba.

II

Although Miguel de Unamuno was recently condemned to fifteen years' imprisonment for *lèse majesté* for some remark made in an article published in a Valencia paper, no attempt has been made either to make him serve the term or to remove him from the chair of Greek at the University of Salamanca. Which proves something about the efficiency of the stand Giner de los Ríos and his friends made fifty years before. Furthermore, at the time of the revolutionary attempt of August, 1917, the removal of Bestiero from his chair caused so many of the faculty to resign and such universal protest that he was reinstated although an actual member of the revolutionary committee and at that time under sentence for life. In 1875 after the fall of the republic it had been in the face of universal popular reaction that the Krausistas founded their free university. The lump is leavened.

But Unamuno. A Basque from the country of Loyola, living in Salamanca in the highest coldest part of the plateau of old Castile, in many senses the opposite of Giner de los Ríos, who was austere as a man on a long pleasant walk doesn't overeat or overdrink so that the walk may be longer and pleasanter, while Unamuno is austere religiously, mystically. Giner de los Ríos was the champion of life, Unamuno is the champion of death. Here is his creed, one of his creeds, from the preface of the *Vida de Don Quijote y Sancho*:

"There is no future: there is never a future. This thing they call the future is one of the greatest lies. Today is the real future. What will we be tomorrow? There is no tomorrow. What about us today, now; that is the only question."

"And as for today, all these nincompoops are thoroughly satisfied because they exist today, mere existence is enough for them. Existence, ordinary naked existence fills their whole soul. They feel nothing beyond existence."

"But do they exist? Really exist? I think not, because if they did exist, if they really existed, existence would be suffering for them and they wouldn't content themselves with it. If they really and truly existed in time and space they would suffer not being of eternity and infinity. And this suffering, this passion, what is it but the passion of God in us? God who suffers in us from our temporariness and finitude, that divine suffering will burst all the puny bonds of logic with which they try to tie down their puny memories and their puny hopes, the illusion of their past and the illusion of their future."

"Your Quixotic madness has made you more than once speak to me of Quixotism as the new religion. And I tell you that this new religion you propose to me, if it hatched, would have two singular merits. One that its founder, its prophet, Don Quixote—not Cervantes—probably wasn't a real man of flesh and blood at all, indeed we suspect that he was pure fiction. And the other merit would be that this prophet was a ridiculous prophet, people's butt and laughing stock.

"What we need most is the valor to face ridicule. Ridicule is the arm of all the miserable barbers, bachelors, parish priests, canons and dukes who keep hidden the sepulchre of the Knight of Madness, Knight who made all the world laugh but never cracked a joke. He had too great a soul to bring forth jokes. They laughed at his seriousness."

"Begin then, friend, to do as Peter the Hermit and call people to join you, to join us, and let us all go win back the sepulchre even if we don't know where it is. The crusade itself will reveal to us the sacred place."

"Start marching! Where are you going? The star will tell you: to the sepulchre! What shall we do on the road while we march? What? Fight! Fight, and how?"

"How? If you find a man lying? Shout in his face: 'lie!' and forward! If you find a man stealing, shout: 'thief!' and forward! If you find a man babbling asininities, to whom the crowd listens open-mouthed, shout at them all: 'idiots!' and forward, always forward!"

"To the march then! And throw out of the sacred squadron all those who begin to study the step and its length and its rhythm. Above everything, throw out all those who fuss about this business of rhythm. They'll turn the squadron into a quadrille and the march into a dance. Away with them! Let them go off somewhere else to sing the flesh."

"Those who try to turn the squadron on the march into a dancing quadrille call themselves and each other poets. But they're not.

They're something else. They only go to the sepulchre out of curiosity, to see what it's like, looking for a new sensation, and to amuse themselves along the road. Away with them!"

"It's these that with their indulgence of Bohemians contribute to maintain cowardice and lies and all the weaknesses that flood us. When they preach liberty they only think of one: that of disposing of their neighbor's wife. All is sensuality with them. They even fall in love sensually with ideas, with great ideas. They are incapable of marrying a great and pure idea and breeding a family with it; they only flirt with ideas. They want them as mistresses, sometimes just for the night. Away with them!"

"If a man wants to pluck some flower or other along the path that smiles from the fringe of grass, let him pluck it, but without breaking ranks, without dropping out of the squadron of which the leader must always keep his eyes on the flaming sonorous star. But if he put the little flower in the strap above his cuirass, not to look at it himself, but for others to look at, away with him! Let him go with his flower in his buttonhole and dance somewhere else."

"Look, friend, if you want to accomplish your mission and serve your country you must make yourself unpleasant to the sensitive boys who only see the world through the eyes of their sweethearts. Or through something worse. Let your words be strident and rasping in their ears."

"The squadron must only stop at night, near a wood or under the lee of a mountain. There they will pitch their tents and the crusaders will wash their feet, and sup off what their women have prepared, then they will beget a son on them and kiss them and go to sleep to begin the march again the following day. And when someone dies they will leave him on the edge of the road with his armor on him, at the mercy of the crows. Let the dead take the trouble to bury the dead."

Instead of the rationalists and humanists of the North, Unamuno's idols are the mystics and saints and sensualists of

Castile, hard stalwart men who walked with God, Loyola, Torquemada, Pizarro, Narváez, who governed with whips and thumbscrews and drank death down greedily like heady wine. He is excited by the amorous madness of the mysticism of Santa Teresa and San Juan de la Cruz. His religion is paradoxical, unreasonable, of faith alone, full of furious yearning other-worldliness. His style, it follows perforce, is headlong, gruff, redundant, full of tremendous pounding phrases. There is a vigorous angry insistence about his dogmas that makes his essays unforgettable, even if one objects as violently as I do to his asceticism and death-worship. There is an anarchic fury about his crying in the wilderness that will win many a man from the fleshpots and chain gangs.

In the apse of the old cathedral of Salamanca is a fresco of the Last Judgment, perhaps by the Castilian painter Gallegos. Over the retablo on a black ground a tremendous figure of the avenging angel brandishes a sword while behind him unrolls the scroll of the *Dies Irae* and huddled clusters of plump little naked people fall away into space from under his feet. There are moments in *"Del Sentimiento Trágico de la Vida"* and in the *"Vida de Don Quijote y Sancho"* when in the rolling earthy Castilian phrases one can feel the brandishing of the sword of that very angel. Not for nothing does Unamuno live in the rust and saffron-colored town of Salamanca in the midst of bare red hills that bulge against an enormous flat sky in which the clouds look like piles of granite, like floating cathedrals, they are so solid, heavy, ominous. A country where barrenness and the sweep of cold wind and the lash of strong wine have made people's minds ingrow into the hereafter, where the clouds have been tramped by the angry feet of the destroying angel. A Patmos for a new Apocalypse. Unamuno is constantly attacking sturdily those who clamor for the modernization, Europeanization of Spanish life and Spanish thought: he is the counterpoise to the northward-yearning apostles of Giner de los Ríos.

In an essay in one of the volumes published by the *Residencia de Estudiantes* he wrote:

"As can be seen I proceed by what they call arbitrary affirmations, without documentation, without proof, outside of a modern European logic, disdainful of its methods."

"Perhaps. I want no other method than that of passion, and when my breast swells with disgust, repugnance, sympathy or disdain, I let the mouth speak the bitterness of the heart, and let the words come as they come."

"We Spaniards are, they say, arbitrary charlatans, who fill up with rhetoric the gaps in logic, who subtilize with more or less ingenuity, but uselessly, who lack the sense of coherence, with scholastic souls, casuists and all that."

"I've heard similar things said of Augustine, the great African, soul of fire that spilt itself in leaping waves of rhetoric, twistings of the phrase, antithesis, paradoxes and ingenuities. Saint Augustine was a Gongorine and a conceptualist at the same time, which makes me think that Gongorism and conceptualism are the most natural forms of passion and vehemence."

"The great African, the great ancient African! Here is an expression—ancient African—that one can oppose to modern European, and that's worth as much at least. African and ancient were Saint Augustine and Tertullian. And why shouldn't we say: 'We must make ourselves ancient African-style' or else 'We must make ourselves African ancient-style.'"

The typical tree of Castile is the encina, a kind of live-oak that grows low with dense bluish foliage and a ribbed, knotted and contorted trunk; it always grows singly and on dry hills. On the roads one meets lean men with knotted hands and brown sun-wizened faces that seem brothers to the encinas of their country. The thought of Unamuno, emphatic, lonely, contorted, hammered into homely violent phrases, oak-tough, oak-twisted, is brother to the men on the roads and to the encinas on the hills of Castile.

This from the end of *"Del Sentimiento Trágico de la Vida"*:

"And in this critical century, Don Quixote has also contaminated himself with criticism, and he must charge against himself, victim of intellectualism and sentimentalism, who when he is most sincere appears most affected. The poor man wants to rationalize the irrational, and irrationalize the rational. And he falls victim of the inevitable despair of a rationalism century, of which the greatest victims were Tolstoy and Nietzsche. Out of despair he enters into the heroic fury of that Quixote of thought who broke out of the cloister, Giordano Bruno, and makes himself awakener of sleeping souls, '*dormitantium animorum excubitor,*' as the ex-Dominican says of himself, he who wrote: 'Heroic love is proper to superior natures called insane—*insane*, not because they do not know—*non sanno*—but because they know too much—*soprasanno*—.'"

"But Bruno believed in the triumph of his doctrines, or at least at the foot of his statue on the Campo dei Fiori, opposite the Vatican, they have put that it is offered by the century he had divined—'*il secolo da lui divinato.*' But our Don Quixote, the resurrected, internal Don Quixote, does not believe that his doctrines will triumph in the world, because they are not his. And it is better that they should not triumph. If they wanted to make Don Quixote king he would retire alone to the hilltop, fleeing the crowds of king-makers and king-killers, as did Christ when, after the miracle of the loaves and fishes, they wanted to proclaim him king. He left the title of king to be put above the cross."

"What is, then, the new mission of Don Quixote in this world? To cry, to cry in the wilderness. For the wilderness hears although men do not hear, and one day will turn into a sonorous wood, and that solitary voice that spreads in the desert like seed will sprout into a gigantic cedar that will sing with a hundred thousand tongues an eternal hosanna to the Lord of life and death."

XVII

"Lyaeus, you've found it."

"Her, you mean."

"No, the essence, the gesture."

"I carry no butterfly net."

The sun blazed in a halo of heat about their heads. Both sides of the straight road olive trees contorted gouty trunks as they walked past. On a bank beside a quietly grazing donkey a man was asleep wrapped in a brown blanket. Occasionally a little grey bird twittered encouragingly from the telegraph wires. When the wind came there was a chill of winter and wisps of cloud drifted across the sun and a shiver of silver ran along the olive groves.

"Tel," cried Lyaeus after a pause, "maybe I have found it. Maybe you are right. You should have been with me last night."

"What happened last night?" As a wave of bitter envy swept over him Telemachus saw for a moment the face of his mother Penelope, brows contracted with warning, white hand raised in admonition. For a fleeting second the memory of his quest brushed through the back of his mind. But Lyaeus was talking.

"Nothing much happened. There were a few things…. O this is wonderful." He waved a clenched fist about his head. "The finest people, Tel! You never saw such people, Tel. They gave me a tambourine. Here it is; wait a minute." He placed the bag he carried on his shoulder on top of a milestone and untied its mouth. When he pulled the tambourine out it was full of figs. "Look, pocket these. I taught her to write her name on the back; see, 'Pilar,' She didn't know how to write."

Telemachus involuntarily cleared his throat.

"It was the finest dive ... Part house, part cave. We all roared in and there was the funniest little girl ... Lot of other people, fat women, but my eyes were in a highly selective state. She was very skinny with enormous black eyes, doe's eyes, timid as a dog's. She had a fat pink puppy in her lap."

"But I meant something in line, movement, eternal, not that."

"There are very few gestures," said Lyaeus.

They walked along in silence.

"I am tired," said Lyaeus; "at least let's stop in here. I see a bush over the door."

"Why stop? We are nearly there."

"Why go on?"

"We want to get to Toledo, don't we?"

"Why?"

"Because we started for there."

"No reason at all," said Lyaeus with a laugh as he went in the door of the wineshop.

When they came out they found Don Alonso waiting for them, holding his horse by the bridle.

"The Spartans," he said with a smile, "never drank wine on the march."

"How far are we from Toledo?" asked Telemachus. "It was nice of you to wait for us."

"About a league, five kilometers, nothing.... I wanted to see your faces when you first saw the town. I think you will appreciate it."

"Let's walk fast," said Telemachus. "There are some things one doesn't want to wait for."

"It will be sunset and the whole town will be on the paseo in front of the hospital of San Juan Bautista.... This is Sunday of Carnival; people will be dressed up in masks and very noisy. It's a day on which they play tricks on strangers."

"Here's the trick they played me at the last town," said Lyaeus agitating his bag of figs. "Let's eat some. I'm sure the Spartans ate figs on the road. Will Rosinante,—I mean will your horse eat them?" He put his hand with some figs on it under the horse's mouth. The horse sniffed noisily out of black nostrils dappled with pink and then reached for the figs. Lyaeus wiped his hand on the seat of his pants and they proceeded.

"Toledo is symbolically the soul of Spain," began Don Alonso after a few moments of silent walking. "By that I mean that through the many Spains you have seen and will see is everywhere an undercurrent of fantastic tragedy, Greco on the one hand, Goya on the other, Moráles, Gallegos, a great flame of despair amid dust, rags, ulcers, human life rising in a sudden pæan out of desolate abandoned dun-colored spaces. To me, Toledo expresses the supreme beauty of that tragic farce.... And the apex, the victory, the deathlessness of it is in El Greco.... How strange it is that it should be that Cypriote who lived in such Venetian state in a great house near the abandoned synagogue, scandalizing us austere Spaniards by the sounds of revelry and unabashed music that came from it at meal-times, making pert sayings under the nose of humorless visitors like Pacheco, living solitary in a country where he remained to his death misunderstood and alien and where two centuries thought of him along with Don Quixote as a madman,—how strange that it should be he who should express most flamingly all that was imperturbable in Toledo.... I have often wondered whether that fiery vitality of spirit that we feel in El Greco, that we felt in my generation when I was young, that I see occasionally in the young men of your time, has become conscious only because it is about to be smothered in the great advancing waves of European banality. I was thinking the other day that perhaps states of life only became conscious once their intensity was waning."

"But most of the intellectuals I met in Madrid," put in Telemachus, "seemed enormously anxious for subways and mechanical progress, seemed to think that existence could be made perfect by slot-machines."

"They are anxious to hold stock in the subway and slot-machine enterprises that they may have more money to unSpanish themselves in Paris ... but let us not talk of that. From the next turn in the road, round that little hill, we shall see Toledo."

Don Alonso jumped on his horse, and Lyaeus and Telemachus doubled the speed of their stride.

First above the bulge of reddish saffron striped with dark of a plowed field they saw a weathercock, then under it the slate cap of a tower. "The Alcázar," said Don Alonso. The road turned away and olive trees hid the weathercock. At the next bend the towers were four, strongly buttressing a square building where on the western windows glinted reflections of sunset. As they walked more towers, dust colored, and domes and the spire of a cathedral, greenish, spiky like the tail of a pickerel, jutted to the right of the citadel. The road dipped again, passed some white houses where children sat in the doorways; from the inner rooms came a sound of frying oil and a pungence of cistus-twigs burning. Starting up the next rise that skirted a slope planted with almond trees they caught sight of a castle, rounded towers, built of rough grey stone, joined by crenellated walls that appeared occasionally behind the erratic lacework of angular twigs on which here and there a cluster of pink flowers had already come into bloom. At the summit was a wineshop with mules tethered against the walls, and below the Tagus and the great bridge, and Toledo.

Against the grey and ochre-streaked theatre of the Cigarrales were piled masses of buttressed wall that caught the orange sunset light on many tall plane surfaces rising into crenellations and square towers and domes and slate-capped spires above a litter of yellowish tile roofs that fell away in terraces from the highest points and sloped outside the walls towards the river and the piers from which sprang the enormous arch of the bridge. The shadows were blue-green and violet. A pale cobalt haze of supperfires hung over the quarters near the river. As they started down the hill towards the heavy pile of San Juan Bautista, that stood under its broad tiled dome outside the nearest gate, a great volley of bell-ringing swung about their ears. A donkey brayed; there was a sound of shouting from the town.

"Here we are, gentlemen, I'll look for you tomorrow at the *fonda*," shouted Don Alonso. He took off his hat and galloped towards the gate, leaving Telemachus and Lyaeus standing by the roadside looking out over the city.

Beyond the zinc bar was an irregular room with Nile-green walls into which light still filtered through three little round arches high up on one side. In a corner were some hogsheads of wine, in another small tables with three-legged stools. From outside came the distant braying of a brass band and racket of a street full of people, laughter, and the occasional shivering jangle of a tambourine. Lyaeus had dropped onto a stool and spread his feet out before him on the tiled floor.

"Never walked so far in my life," he said, "my toes are pulverized, pulverized!" He leaned over and pulled off his shoes. There were holes in his socks. He pulled them off in turn, and started wiggling his toes meditatively. His ankles were grimed with dust.

"Well...." began Telemachus.

The *padrón*, a lean man with moustaches and a fancy yellow vest which he wore unbuttoned over a lavender shirt, brought two glasses of dense black wine.

"You have walked a long way?" he asked, looking with interest at Lyaeus' feet.

"From Madrid."

"*¡Carai!*"

"Not all in one day."

"You are sailors going to rejoin your ship in Sevilla." The *padrón* looked from one to another with a knowing expression, twisting his mouth so that one of the points of his moustache slanted towards the ceiling and the other towards the floor.

"Not exactly...."

Another man drew up his chair to their table, first taking off his wide cap and saying gravely: "*Con permiso de ustedes.*" His broad, slightly flabby face was very pale; the eyes under his sparse blonde eyelashes were large and grey. He put his two hands on their shoulders so as to draw their heads together and said in a whisper:

"You aren't deserters, are you?"

"No."

"I hoped you were. I might have helped you. I escaped from prison in Barcelona a week ago. I am a syndicalist."

"Have a drink," cried Lyaeus. "Another glass.... And we can let you have some money if you need it, too, if you want to get out of the country."

The *padrón* brought the wine and retired discreetly to a chair beside the bar from which he beamed at them with almost religious approbation.

"You are comrades?"

"Of those who break out," said Lyaeus flushing. "What about the progress of events? When do you think the pot will boil over?"

"Soon or never," said the syndicalist.... "That is never in our lifetime. We are being buried under industrialism like the rest of Europe. Our people, our comrades even, are fast getting the bourgeois mentality. There is danger that we shall lose everything we have fought for.... You see, if we could only have captured the means of production when the system was young and weak, we could have developed it slowly for our benefit, made the machine the slave of man. Every day we wait makes it more difficult. It is a race as to whether this peninsula will be captured by communism or capitalism. It is still neither one nor the other, in its soul." He thumped his clenched fist against his chest.

"How long were you in prison?"

"Only a month this time, but if they catch me it will be bad. They won't catch me."

He spoke quietly without gestures, occasionally rolling an unlit cigarette between his brown fingers.

"Hadn't we better go out before it gets quite dark?" said Telemachus.

"When shall I see you again?" said Lyaeus to the syndicalist.

"Oh, we'll meet if you stay in Toledo a few days...."

Lyaeus got to his feet and took the man by the arm.

"Look, let me give you some money; won't you be wanting to go to Portugal?"

The man flushed and shook his head.

"If our opinions coincided...."

"I agree with all those who break out," said Lyaeus.

"That's not the same, my friend."

They shook hands and Telemachus and Lyaeus went out of the tavern.

Two carriages hung with gaudily embroidered shawls, full of dominos and pierrots and harlequins who threw handfuls of confetti at people along the sidewalks, clattered into town through the dark arches of the gate. Telemachus got some confetti in his mouth. A crowd of little children danced about him jeering as he stood spluttering on the curbstone. Lyaeus took him by the arm and drew him along the street after the carriages, bent double with laughter. This irritated Telemachus who tore his arm away suddenly and made off with long strides up a dark street.

A half-waned moon shone through the perforations in a round terra-cotta chimney into the street's angular greenish shadow. From somewhere came the seethe of water over a dam. Telemachus was leaning against a damp wall, tired and exultant, looking vaguely at the oval of a woman's face half surmised behind the bars of an upper window, when he heard a clatter of unsteady feet on the cobbles and Lyaeus appeared, reeling a little, his lips moist, his eyebrows raised in an expression of drunken jollity.

"Lyaeus, I am very happy," cried Telemachus stepping forward to meet his friend. "Walking about here in these empty zigzag streets I have suddenly felt familiar with it all, as if it were a part of me, as if I had soaked up some essence out of it."

"Silly that about essences, gestures, Tel, silly.... Awake all you need." Lyaeus stood on a little worn stone that kept wheels off the corner of the house where the street turned and waved his arms. "Awake! *Dormitant animorum excubitor*…. That's not right. Latin's no good. Means a fellow who says: 'wake up, you son of a gun.'"

"Oh, you're drunk. It's much more important than that. It's like learning to swim. For a long time you flounder about, it's unpleasant and gets up your nose and you choke. Then all at once you are swimming like a duck. That's how I feel about all this…. The challenge was that woman in Madrid, dancing, dancing…."

"Tel, there are things too good to talk about…. Look, I'm like St. Simeon Stylites." Lyaeus lifted one leg, then the other, waving his arms like a tight-rope walker.

"When I left you I walked out over the other bridge, the bridge of St. Martin and climbed…."

"Shut up, I think I hear a girl giggling up in the window there."

Lyaeus stood up very straight on his column and threw a kiss up into the darkness. The giggling turned to a shrill laughter; a head craned out from a window opposite. Lyaeus beckoned with both hands.

"Never mind about them…. Look out, somebody threw something…. Oh, it's an orange…. I want to tell you how I felt the gesture. I had climbed up on one of the hills of the Cigarrales and was looking at the silhouette of the town so black against the stormy marbled sky. The moon hadn't risen yet…. Let's move away from here."

"*Ven, flor de mi corazón*," shouted Lyaeus towards the upper window.

"A flock of goats was passing on the road below, and from somewhere came the tremendous lilt of…."

"Heads!" cried Lyaeus throwing himself round an angle in the wall.

Telemachus looked up, his mind full of his mother Penelope's voice saying reproachfully:

"You might have been murdered in that dark alley." A girl was leaning from the window, shaken with laughter, taking aim with a bucket she swung with both hands.

"Stop," cried Telemachus, "it's the other...."

As he spoke a column of cold water struck his head, knocked his breath out, drenched him.

"Speaking of gestures...." whispered Lyaeus breathlessly from the doorway where he was crouching, and the street was filled with uncontrollable shrieking laughter.